ᴎ

JUDGE COLT

The South Desert country was subject to recurrent and violent trouble. Constable Mulligan of Stillwater did not favour the law as administered by Judge Colt and tried to give every man a fair trial. Before the dust settled, however, Mulligan came to the conclusion that Judge Colt's kind of justice, bloody though it might be, was at least in some situations preferable to the law of the land. And there was no appeal!

BUCK BRADSHAW

JUDGE COLT

Complete and Unabridged

LINFORD
Leicester

First published in Great Britain in 1995 by
Robert Hale Limited
London

First Linford Edition
published 1996
by arrangement with
Robert Hale Limited
London

British Library CIP Data

Bradshaw, Buck
    Judge Colt.—Large print ed.—
    Linford western library
    1. English fiction—20th century
    2. Large type books
    I. Title
    823.9′14 [F]

    ISBN 0–7089–7954–8

Published by
F. A. Thorpe (Publishing) Ltd.
Anstey, Leicestershire

Set by Words & Graphics Ltd.
Anstey, Leicestershire
Printed and bound in Great Britain by
T. J. Press (Padstow) Ltd., Padstow, Cornwall

This book is printed on acid-free paper

1

The World of Jawn Henry Mulligan

SIXTO ERRO was a big-boned individual who carried his weight well. He was somewhat less than average height, had coal-black eyes, a barrel chest, could lift a half-grown steer on his shoulders, had a mouthful of dazzling white teeth and a smile that would melt the heart of an iron monkey.

His age was indeterminate; people of Sixto Erro's background showed age slowly. His grandfather, who had been a Basque, died in bed at ninety-six without a grey hair in his head.

It was said in Mex-town, which was the original village of Stillwater, that Sixto had to be at least sixty. This reasoning was based on the fact that Sixto'd had four wives.

1

In Gringo-town, which was a two-sided roadway created after New Mexico Territory was acquired by the United States of the North in 1848 with the Treaty of Guadalupe, whose buildings showed their backs to Mex-town, it was said Sixto Erro was the enigma of enigmas because he spoke accentless English, and while the colour of sun-hardened leather, except for his broad smile, thought and acted like a gringo.

Sixto's fourth wife, much younger than her husband, was a slight woman with a backbone of iron and the disposition of a saint. She was pretty, and on a good day could charm a bird down out of a tree. Her name was Elena. Her father had been a de Echevarria, member of Mexican aristocracy, people whose fortunes and standing fluctuated predictably after the coming of Benito Juarez. He had fled Mexico, had settled in the village of Stillwater in the United States of the North without money, influence or any particular social standing.

He had died embittered. His better moments had been at Juan Sosa's cantina where inexpensive red wine had the capability of inducing hallucinogenic recollections of better days.

Sixto the son-in-law had a great heart. He was an accomplished horseman, a lover of life — and women. God alone knew how many children he'd produced from his three wives, but none from Elena, the fourth wife.

His residence in Mex-town had four rooms, a mansion in comparison to other *jacals*. He had a faggot-fenced corral for animals, which included the ubiquitous milk-goat, runty half-wild chickens, a splendid black horse and two jenny mules — the small variety indigenous to Mexico, tough, more durable than the large Missouri *Americano* mules, and inclined to be both opinionated and independent. Ordinarily mules were notorious for kicking. Sixto's mules bit.

The constable of Stillwater, Jawn

Henry Mulligan, was 'new' to the South-west, having only been there eleven years. Unlike most of the residents of Gringo-town he visited Mex-town as often as he could. His job required him to maintain order in Stillwater, which ordinarily encompassed regulating the behaviour of rangemen in from the cow-camps which, in hereditary fashion, were maintained some distance from the town, and operated by cowmen who drove cattle into the South Desert for the two or three months of flourishing, nourishing feed of springtime, then left after the graze and browse withered, driving back north where summer and autumn feed was regenerated through rainfall, something which was rare on the desert after May.

Jawn Henry was a bulky individual with a weathered-dark face, fists of granite and the variety of size that had an intimidating effect.

Jawn Henry was pleasant, but just below the surface was a different Jawn

Henry. It was due more to the latter than the former that he had kept his job all those years.

It was said he had once broken the back of a fighting wild stallion with one blow; highly unlikely, but the South-west throve on magnificent exaggerations, twice-life-size myths and dolorous sagas of unrequited love, heroic brigandage, splendid stories of exalted vengeance — and miracles.

In Gringo-town established merchants, as well as residents, accepted the myths and mysticism of Mex-town with a shrug and no comment. People were entitled to believe as they wished to believe; in Gringo-town it was trade and commerce. Huge wagons rolled through Stillwater more often in winter and springtime than in summer; they were vehicles with tyres six inches wide to prevent unnecessary sinking into sand and soft earth under heavy loads. Stillwater had two public corrals where freighters could rest animals and drovers could camp.

Everyone benefited, from the town blacksmith to the mercantile's proprietor, to the hotelman whose ramshackle converted army barracks had cubbyhole rooms with minimal furnishings to accommodate men who slept in their boots and clothing.

The saddle and harness works benefited, as did the tiny apothecary shop sandwiched between the saloon and mercantile.

The liveryman benefited least. Drovers carried their own feed, used the public corrals at the north end of town, and rarely bought or traded animals at the trading — and livery — barn.

There was no paradise on earth like the South Desert in springtime; the air was perfumed, grass throve from warm rains, flowers flourished, the sky was a flawless turquoise-blue, and human activity which had been more or less town-bound through bitter, windy winters, came forth to put into execution the dreams and schemes hatched during house-bound winters. It was this fact which made commerce flourish, brought the drovers south, and which also gave Jawn Henry Mulligan his occasional reasons to leave town armed to the gills because, while the US Army governed territories, it was unable to police an area larger than almost any two states — excluding Texas — in the national union, inhabited by a polyglot of skin-tones ranging from lily white through an almost interminable spectrum of browns, whose customs, attire, language and other facts, such as religion and philosophy, were endlessly varied.

Jawn Henry lived in this environment as any sensible man would have: he ignored, insofar as it was possible, everything except administration of the law, as he and most others interpreted it, which actually had less to do with legalese than with basic justice.

Raised a confirmed Southern Baptist, Jawn Henry's particular friend was a Jesuit, Father Ignacio Ruiz, who was not in the strictest sense a Mexican.

He was what Mexicans derisively called a 'gachupin', meaning simply 'one who wears spurs', but the term went three hundred years deeper than that; Spaniards who conquered Latin-America wore spurs. To be called a gachupin was either to be insulted, or, as with Sixto Erro who always smiled, a form of teasing, not an insult. The smile made the difference.

Gachupins were frequently people of pure Spanish descent, whether born in Iberia or Mexico. Father Ignacio Ruiz was a *Criollo*, someone of pure Spanish descent born in Mexico instead of Spain.

Father Ruiz was a gnome of sixty, built like a bird with fine bones and yet surprisingly durable and physically tireless as well as strong. He was the most recent priest at *San Felipe de Catolica*, the dilapidated old mission which rose higher even than the wooden buildings of Gringo-town, had walls three feet thick of adobe, an askew wooden cross above the entry and

8

several very high, narrow windows, made that way so that Indians could not shoot people at prayer in the days when half a dozen varieties of neolithics, but predominantly Apaches, contested ownership of the territory.

It was Father Ruiz who brought to the Gringo-town office and jailhouse of Constable Jawn Henry the problem which was to have reverberations long after the dust had settled, and he did it innocently.

He sat in the chair with the hem of his robe stained from walking through dirt and dust, contemplated his plain black footwear and said, "Do you know a man named Raine Cotswol?"

The constable nodded. He knew Raine Cotswol well; better in fact than he knew most of the other northerly cowmen who drove herds to the South Desert each spring.

"A rider of his named Carl Maxwell stole a horse from an old man in Mextown who catches wild ones, breaks them to saddle and sells them."

The constable was impassive when he said, "What old man?"

"Carlos Aguirre. Do you know him?"

The constable nodded. He had known Aguirre since he'd come into the country. He was one of those ageless individuals who were the colour of old leather and twice as tough.

"How do you know Cotswol's rider stole the horse?"

Father Ruiz finally raised his eyes. "Carlos saw him catch the horse and lead it away. So did others. Only three or four knew this Cotswol rider by sight but they all knew the Circle R brand on his horse."

Jawn Henry stared. "In broad daylight?"

"Yes," the priest replied, continuing to regard the other man. "That bothered me, too. A man on a branded horse some of the people recognized, rode — in broad daylight — where a horse was tied out, cut the rope and led the horse away." Father Ruiz's forehead puckered. "It makes no sense, Jawn

Henry, which is why I came to see you . . . horse-thieves come in the night."

"Was Carlos positive in his identification of that Cotswol rider?"

"Of a certainty. He was sitting under his *ramada* out back."

"When?"

"Yesterday before supper. About four o'clock in the afternoon. He saw the rider approach out where he had staked the horse, dismount, cut the rope, mount and lead the horse away."

"An' he just sat there, father?"

"The horse was staked out a-ways. There hasn't been any grass close to Mex-town in months." The priest arose. "I thought about it last night. It was almost as though that rangeman wanted to be seen . . . it made no sense to me, does it to you?"

Jawn Henry shook his head and arose as the priest went to the door and hesitated there, looking back as the constable spoke. "I'll talk to Carlos."

"Yes. But I wonder . . . did this Cotswol rider steal the horse like that because he was going to leave the country? He wouldn't take the horse then ride back to the Cotswol camp with it — not when so many people saw him take the animal."

Jawn Henry said, "I'll ride out to the Cotswol place later."

After the priest departed Jawn Henry remained standing. Horse-thieves were a dime a dozen, but he'd never known one to do as that Cotswol rider had done — in broad daylight, with people watching. He sat down, rolled and lighted a smoke, and made a wry face. One thing was a blessed fact: run-of-the-mill cowboys didn't have the sense God had given a goose. But this had to be the absolute epitome of stupidity — or something else?

Jawn Henry was less interested in how the theft had been accomplished than why it had.

Later, when the sun was low, he went down to Mex-town, found Carlos Aguirre at the adobe cantina, with its one windowless wall-opening facing the plaza, took him outside to a bench and asked questions. Aguirre was old and wiry, very dark with bird-like bright small black eyes, very few teeth, and over the generations had acquired innumerable relatives although he had no children of his own. In fact his wife had died many years earlier, not long after they had been married and had not been able to have children.

With rocks in his pockets he did not weigh a hundred and fifty pounds. His command of English was good enough. Not as good as the English of Father Ruiz although both were the orphaned products of a mission-school where all 13 wards were taught English first, other things second.

Carlos reiterated what had happened in almost identical words the priest had used. Yes, he had recognized the thief, not as well as he recognized the Cotswol brand, but of a certainty well enough to identify him.

The same thing bothered Carlos that had bothered Father Ruiz, and undoubtedly others, and which intrigued Jawn Henry Mulligan. A horse-thief had to be stupid or drunk, or maybe stupid-drunk, to steal a horse in broad daylight near a town where people would see him do it.

The constable asked about the horse. It was like pulling a plug. "He stood between fifteen an' sixteen hands, had good neck and shoulders. He was strong, which is why I went about breaking him slowly . . . carefully, in fact."

"Was he broke to ride?" he asked the old man.

"I rode him three times. He wasn't an old horse, constable. He bucked — just crow-hopped really, like he almost did not want to fight. Yes, he could be rode." Aguirre paused to watch two cocks fight and raise dust several yards distant. When the battle ended with one rooster fleeing for his life, he resumed speaking. "I've been trapping wild ones for more years than you are old. Mostly, they fight and buck if you let them. But this horse," the old man swung his attention to the constable, "there wasn't a mark on him anywhere that he'd been rode, but I'd almost bet new money he had been — green-rode anyway. He didn't respond to reins. I had to squaw-rein him. He was big and strong, seven years old — in his prime — strong and handsome an' savvy. I don't like losing him, constable. Somewhere is a man made to match that horse. I figured to ride him until he come along, an' get good money for him."

"Did you trap him wild, Carlos?" the constable asked.

"Yes. He was alone. He'd wanted to join a band but a stallion ran him off. He walked into one of my faggot corrals and I had him."

Carlos pushed out dusty footwear and contemplated it. "It baffles me," he said, reverting to his native tongue, border Mex-Spanish. "As the priest said . . . in broad daylight when people closest came outside and watched the whole thing. I'd guess the only thing he didn't do was wave as he rode westward in the direction of the Cotswol camp. Tell me, Jawn Henry, does Gringo-law say a man can do such a thing?"

Jawn Henry's reply was given in the straightforward, direct way he thought and usually spoke. He said, "There's no law as far as I know that says folks can steal horses . . . 'specially in daylight with half a village watchin' 'em do it."

Aguirre's black eyes were fixed on the constable as Jawn Henry also said, "Cotswol's got quite a band of riders. I know him pretty well. I don't believe he'd allow anything like this. As little as I know right now, I'd have to say his rider stole that horse on his own."

The constable had an early supper; even so it was quite a distance to the Cotswol cow-camp. He decided to go out there first thing in the morning, which he almost did. The reason he did not get as early a start as he intended was because one of the local stage company's four-in-hands arrived just ahead of dawn with two agitated passengers and a thoroughly disgusted driver who had complained when the company had stopped using gun-guards because there hadn't been a stage stopped in two years.

This coach had been stopped, passengers and whip cleaned out, and sent on its way. The highwayman was out front but the whip and both passengers — drummers, one peddling hardware, the other peddling bolt-goods — swore they saw two gun-barrels aimed in their direction from some boulders on the west side of the road.

To resolve his dual dilemmas Jawn Henry rode through the dog-leg road-bed where pines were close to the pond on both sides, which was where the hold-up had occurred. He found horse-sign of one animal, boot-tracks of one man, and the place where the highwayman had waited in the rocks leaving behind four quirley-butts.

There were shod-horse tracks of one

man leaving the area westerly through the rocks. So much for the conviction about three of them.

Jawn Henry left the area riding south-westerly in the direction of the Cotswol camp with the sun climbing in a world devoid of life except for trickles of cattle he saw now and then.

He wanted to track the highwayman but the stolen horse intrigued him. Not the horse, exactly, but how it had been stolen, and why. If it didn't rain, and the sky was clear, he could pick up the highwayman's tracks tomorrow. The country he had headed into was mostly open grassland and shod horses left tracks easy to distinguish from barefoot horses.

He had Cotswol's cow-camp in sight with the sun directly overhead and no shadows showing except directly under the horse he rode and the occasional brush-clumps and rocks he passed.

In another month or six weeks the heat would make dancing waves, which distorted distances and objects, but for the time being, while there was a hint of the heat to come, it was negligible so Jawn Henry had a pleasant ride all the way to the wagons and general disarray of a cow-camp where nothing had been built because of the temporary nature of the grazing season.

2

The Scent of Trouble

RAINE COTSWOL was standing wide-legged amid the disarray of his cow-camp, hat tipped to shade slaty eyes. Around him were the implements — and the wagon — of camps like his, along with two riders.

He had six riders. The others were out minding cattle. The two in camp were injured, not seriously, but enough to keep them camp-bound for a few days. One had a horse fall with him in a boulder-field, the other one had the quickstep from drinking water.

The riders also watched Jawn Henry. When he was close enough he signalled with an upraised right arm, rode in close, dismounted and offered a hand, which Raine Cotswol shook and released as he spoke.

20

"We're fixin' to eat. Tie the animal an' set."

Jawn Henry trickled reins through one hand, looked steadily at the rawboned, older man and spoke. "How many riders you got, Raine?"

"Six. Tie the horse, we'll — "

"Four out with the cattle?"

Raine Cotswol was a rugged, tough and direct individual. His kind just naturally objected to blunt questions. He now faced the constable with narrowing eyes. "You got somethin' in mind?" he asked.

"Yeah, somethin'. Was all your riders here this morning?"

"Yes, now gawddammit say what you're here for. We got work to do."

Jawn Henry went to work rolling a smoke. The three cowmen watched and waited. When he had lighted up Jawn Henry gave glare for glare with the cowman.

"One more question, Raine. Did one of your riders return to camp leading a horse?"

Cotswol and his two riders looked at lawn Henry as though he'd been kicked in the head by a pigeon. Raine said, "Now why would my riders do such a thing as that?"

"That's what I'm tryin' to find out, Raine. Did one lead a horse back here?"

"Not that I know of. My riders don't need extra mounts. We bring along a *remuda* when we come south."

Jawn Henry loosened, eyed the tripod with the stew-kettle suspended from it and said, "That sure smells good."

Cotswol stood a moment regarding the constable before gesturing. "Then quit talkin', set down an' eat," which Jawn Henry did, and afterwards walked out a-ways with Raine Cotswol to ask another question. "Did you bring the crew with you from up north?"

Again the older man regarded the younger man, irritably this time. "Yes. Four are my year-round men. The other two — well — they hit me up for work on the drive south, an'

I hired 'em . . . Jawn Henry . . . ?"

"There's a horse missin' in town."

"An' you're standin' there sayin' one of my riders is a horse-thief?"

"No sir, not exactly, but he stole it in broad daylight with folks watchin'."

"I see, an' they think it was one of my riders? Which one?"

"I got no idea, but he was ridin' a Cotswol horse. That's why I asked if all your hands had been around today."

Raine stood gazing steadily at the constable. He allowed moments to pass before he spoke again. "I told you they was. Who saw someone steal a horse?"

"Folks in Mex-town."

Cotswol's lip curled. "Jawn Henry, you ought to know better. Messicans believe in *fantasmas*, miracles. You ought to know better. Give me one reason why a rider of mine would steal a horse."

"I got no idea, but a lot of folks saw someone ridin' a Cotswol-branded horse do it, in broad daylight."

"When in broad daylight?"

"Yestiddy. You know where all your riders was, yesterday?"

"The same thing they're doin' today, except those two riders yonder in wagon-shade. Workin' through the cattle. Jawn Henry, I don't like this conversation. I don't hire horse-thieves."

The constable thanked Cotswol for feeding him, got his horse and headed home. The sun was sinking fast. He studied it, decided he'd eat late this evening, and slouched along trying to fit bits and pieces into something that made sense.

Just before entering town he asked his horse a question which elicited no reply. "How does a man know when he's hired a horse-thief?"

The cafeman had been drinking; he was loudly affable as he fed the constable. He was one of those individuals whose disposition seemed to improve with whiskey, and as the constable sat listening to the inanity, he told himself that was most of the time because the cafeman was usually in good spirits, more so after noon than in the morning.

He made one casual remark that heightened Jawn Henry's interest. He said, "You know Sixto Erro?" and when the constable nodded while reaching for his cup of black joe, the cafeman also said, "He got shot yesterday."

Jawn Henry raised his eyes. Sixto Erro was as even-tempered as anyone alive. "What happened?"

"All's I know is what I heard. He was combin' the hills for a horse that was stole from Mex-town, an' someone shot him. He's home. He bled out a lot. That's all I know."

Jawn Henry went over to Mex-town. It was later than he thought; when he knocked on the door of the Erro house Sixto's wife appeared in the doorway, candlelight outlining her from behind. She regarded the constable with a drawn expression. "Not tonight," she said before the lawman had uttered a word. "He is sick."

C-1

"So I heard . . . I'd like to talk to him."

The woman, with dark shadows under each eye, tiredly shook her head. "Not tonight. The *curandera* is with him."

"Did he tell you what happened?"

Elena Erro was becoming impatient. "How could he? He was hanging onto the mane of his horse, blood everywhere. I thank God the horse knew to bring him home . . . excuse me." The woman closed the door.

Jawn Henry turned back in the direction of Gringo-town. He felt tired and he hadn't actually done anything strenuous.

The following morning he arose early, washed and shaved out behind the rooming-house, went down to the cafe and was greeted with a sour look and silence by the cafeman. Jawn Henry ate and moved on.

The news of the shooting was common knowledge. Up at the saloon all manner of speculation was running as free as active, stimulated imaginations could make it.

He listened for a while, exchanged a sardonic wink with the saloonman and went to unlock the *calabozo*.

Father Ruiz came across from the general store, the hem of his robe pale with dust. As he sat down he looked at the constable in silence. Jawn Henry said, "I got an idea is all." The priest waited but that was all Jawn Henry had to say. The priest said he had just come from the Erro place, and paused. Jawn Henry eyed him stoically. "Dead?"

"No, but maybe. He lost much blood . . . why did this happen?"

"God knows," the constable replied dryly, "an' he never says much about these things. Do you know where he was riding?"

"When I was marking the corners of the Cross about daybreak he passed. We nodded but that was all."

"Which way did he go?"

"North out of town at the upper end.

27

I didn't see him beyond that . . . why, Jawn Henry?"

"Want me to guess, padre?"

"Yes."

"It's maybe got somethin' to do with Aguirre's horse."

That's all Jawn Henry said. Later, with heat coming, he returned to the saloon, which was empty of customers except for a snoring old man sitting by the front-wall window.

The saloonman put a glass of beer in front of the constable, picked up the coin and put it into a drawer as he said, "There's been talk of outlaws in the mountains north of here ever since I been around. You reckon Sixto run onto something like that?"

Jawn Henry shrugged, sipped beer and was quiet so long the saloonman went to his tub of greasy water and worked at polishing glass until the constable was departing, then called to him before he reached the roadway door.

"You been up where someone stopped

the coach from up north?"

Jawn Henry had. "Yestiddy. Why?"

"The yardman over yonder ain't happy. Last night he was in here tellin' my customers that you should have gone up there as soon as you heard of the hold-up."

Jawn Henry gazed dispassionately at the saloonman, let the door swing closed and went out behind the jailhouse to see if either of his saddle-animals needed more feed. They didn't. He brought forth one animal, a rawboned, slick chestnut with a flaxen mane and tail, rigged out and left town by the back alley, heading northward.

He hadn't really made a thorough search of the robbery site the previous day. This time he was more relaxed as he went over the area. He made only one discovery, one that in haste he had overlooked the previous day. It was dottle from a pipe amid the trees on the east side of the road; someone had patiently waited over there, the sign was good. Jawn Henry trailed his chestnut by the reins as he criss-crossed the area, and made another discovery. Another man and his horse had been hiding northward about a quarter-mile.

Jawn Henry spent the entire morning sashaying back and forth without finding anything else.

When he was ready to do some tracking the sun was beginning to slant away. Tracks were easy to read in open country, less easy where generations of resin-scented pine needles covered the ground, inhibiting all kinds of underbrush-growth.

It got shadowy before he found the fire-ring where there had been a camp. Because of inhibiting big, tall trees daylight only filtered through. He did not heed time, only timber-gloom.

By the time he desisted and headed back for town he had reached a conclusion. The stager had said there was one outlaw, and two gun-barrels behind him in some rocks.

Yesterday Jawn Henry's cursory,

hasty examination of the site had not been extensive enough; today was different. Whether the robber and his companions ever came down to the road, there still had to be three outlaws, not one.

He left off tracking when it became necessary to lead his horse as he criss-crossed the area.

There may have been more tracks — but not where Jawn Henry had been. What puzzled him was that two of the highwaymen had deliberately remained hidden, and that established the fact beyond question — there had been three, not one.

He struck out for home, had only covered about a mile when a faint reverberation came down the airwaves from a long way off northward.

Jawn Henry halted, twisted to look back and said, "Son of a bitch," before straightening up and continuing on his way.

This time he did not confide in the horse for an excellent reason, he was sunk in thought. When he got back, cared for his animal, had supper and crossed to Mex-town, he needed to talk to Sixto Erro, whether his wife agreed or not.

She did not disagree when he arrived out front of the *jacal*. She led him to the gloomy bedroom where two candles burned. The room had an odd scent to it. Jawn Henry had encountered this before, so had everyone else who lived in the South Desert country — it was the odour of a *curandera's* medicine, distinctly different from the odour of gringo medicine.

Sixto smiled at Jawn Henry, who pulled up a three-legged stool and sat. Sixto's wife hovered in the doorway. Jawn Henry ignored her. He asked how Erro felt and a pair of very dark eyes rolled ceilingward. Sixto did not reply, there was no need. An injured man bedridden from loss of blood, weak as a kitten, did not feel anything but ill.

Jawn Henry asked for details of the shooting and was exasperated by the answer. "What I know, *amigo*, was when I opened my eyes from the ground, the horse was staring at me."

"Did you hear the gun?"

"I just told you. I knew nothing until I opened my eyes."

Jawn Henry made a tactical move. "Where were you — I mean where exactly in the hills were you when you got ambushed?"

"East of Bear Creek on the far side of the road. That's where I was after being shot. Lying on my back. I tied off most of the bleeding, got astride and headed for home. On the way I got out of my head . . . I didn't see the bushwhacker, didn't hear him — and never found Carlos's horse."

Sixto's wife was making small impatient sounds so Jawn Henry stood up, gave Sixto Erro a light slap on the shoulder, and left. He had learned practically nothing. Sixto might be able to be more helpful when he recovered, but on the hike back to Gringo-town, Jawn Henry doubted it.

Someone whose system is shocked by a bullet seemed never afterwards to recall much of the incident. By the time Jawn Henry reached the *juzgado* it was getting cool.

He was preparing to lock up for the night when a solitary rider appeared at the tie-rack, grunted what probably was a greeting, swung off and said, "You got a few minutes?"

Inside, Jawn Henry relighted the hanging-lamp, sat at his table and waited. His visitor was Raine Cotswol looking as solemn as an owl. Eventually the cowman said, "When you was at the camp yestiddy I took it kind of personal, them questions an' that hint you made about me havin' a horse-thief ridin' for me.

Jawn Henry leaned, got comfortable and waited some more.

"Well; there was one rider went out in the mornin' an' none of us has seen him since."

"What's his name?"

"Carl Maxwell."

Jawn Henry nodded which made Raine Cotswol frown. "Him?" he said.

"That's who the Messicans thought it was . . . he didn't come to camp?"

"Nope. Me'n one rider went lookin' for him."

Jawn Henry was tired. He wanted to end this so he said, "Find him?"

"Found horse-tracks which was likely his, except there was four sets of tracks. Jawn Henry, I don't like havin' someone saddlin up one morning an' ridin' one of my horses away without comin' back. We figured he might have got jumped off, but the feller with me, an In'ian called Lame — he ain't lame, I got no idea how he come to be called that — he can read sign off a glass window. He said Carl didn't get bucked off an' hurt. After we'd read sign most of today, Lame went to the edge of them forested hills north, east and west and showed me where the feller ridin' my horse an' two other fellers went right up into the timber like they knew where they was goin'.

We turned back, it was gettin' dark, even Lame can't read sign after dark." The cowman made another of those long pauses before also saying, "We had four sets of marks most of the time."

"Like someone was leading a horse?"

"Yes. An' when I asked around a while back folks told me the same story you told me — about a Cotswol rider stealin' an animal down in Mex-town . . . you reckon that could be the fourth horse?"

"It's possible," the constable said, thinking less of the stolen horse and more about three — not one — highwaymen stopping a south-bound coach.

Raine Cotswol stood up and pulled on his gloves. "I figure to take Lame an' track them fellers in the morning."

Jawn Henry also arose. "Be careful, Raine. You know Sixto Erro?"

"Yes . . . not him?"

"No, he didn't steal the horse but he went lookin' for it in them hills and some bushwhacking son of a bitch shot him."

Cotswol's eyes widened. "Sixto? Is he dead?"

"No, but he's not goin' to dance any fandangos for a long time. He was shot, as near as I can tell, somewhere northward in timber country."

"Who done it?"

"I got no idea. What I'm sayin' is if you ride up into those mountains . . . there's a bushwhacker up there, Raine. If I was you I'd take my whole crew."

"I can't do that. We're fixin' to gather, mark an' brand."

Jawn Henry faced the cowman. "I think this bushwhacker is a pretty good shot . . . if you get yourself killed it won't matter about workin' cattle, will it?"

Cotswol stood gazing at the larger and younger man. "What in hell is this country comin' to?"

"Nothin' it hasn't been all along."

"You want to ride with us? We can

find him an' leave his carcass hangin' from a tree limb."

Jawn Henry sat back down. "You don't want me along if you're goin' to do somethin' like that."

"Why?"

"Why — dammit — because there's laws against lynchin' an' I get paid to see the laws are kept."

Cotswol went as far as the door before speaking again. "A danged horse-thief who bushwhacks someone don't deserve hangin'?"

"Raine, if you find him I don't want to ever hear what you did."

"You think lynchin' this son of a bitch hadn't ought to happen, Jawn Henry?"

"Raine, you're tryin' to put me between a rock and a hard place. I get paid to uphold the damned law . . . hang the son of bitch if you find him an' don't never talk to me about it again . . . but be damned careful. I got a feelin' it's not just one bushwhacker."

"There's more of 'em?"

"I don't know but I think so. Those four horses you'n your In'ian tracked . . . I'm beginnin' to think were ridden by three men, one of which is your rider Maxwell."

After the cowman departed Jawn Henry blew down the lamp-mantle for the second time, locked his jailhouse from out front and hiked up to the rooming-house, too tired to stop at the saloon for a nightcap.

3

Fight!

THE following day passed slowly. Constable Mulligan went back up to the robbery site, retraced the tracks for the second time and from a pine-topped low hillock saw three distant riders loping north in the direction of the hill country and would have bet new money one of them was Raine Cotswol, the other two his riders.

He waited until they were well northward then also rode northward, but only as far as the forest fringe, then sashayed westerly until he cut sign of Cotswol and his companions. He took up the trail from there. If they found a bushwhacker Jawn Henry could discreetly lose himself on the downhill side. If they didn't find him . . . Jawn

Henry wagged his head. What kind of outlaw remained in the same country after stopping a stage?

For a damned fact, why had he bushwhacked Sixto Erro? Two possible reasons came to mind. One, the bushwhacker wasn't ready to abandon the area. Two, Sixto had got too close to someone's camp.

Raine and his riders could be heading into the same situation. Jawn Henry rode a loose rein watching and listening. Sure as Gawd had made green apples, if they were dogging Sixto's tracks or the sign of Maxwell and his companions, they were going to ride into the sights of the same gun-barrel.

It seemed unlikely that anyone as savvy as Raine Cotswol would do such a thing, he'd been around a lot of years, but on the other hand being old was not always the same as being *coyote*.

The tracks were easy to follow, easier than they had been on Jawn Henry's other ride up through here.

It did not occur to the constable until

he was well up-country that Cotswol might have another reason for pushing ahead the way he was doing. His rider named Maxwell had taken a Cotswol horse, which was a lynching offence, but worse in the eyes of rangemen he had betrayed the trust a stockman had put in him, and that was nothing to be considered lightly. It was, Jawn Henry mused, more likely the latter than the former; hell, Cotswol had plenty of horses, losing one to a thief would be bitter to live with but it would not stack up to betraying a trust.

It became warm in the timber; sunlight rarely reached through bristly pine and fir tops but heat did. Not as noticeable in timber-country as it would be in grassland-country, but pleasant enough to make a man sag comfortably in the saddle, which was what Jawn Henry was doing when the flat sound of a gunshot broke the hush up ahead and seemingly to the east.

Jawn Henry snapped upright in the saddle. His initial response was to hasten forward. Instinct warned him to make slow progress, very slow progress, which was what he did.

When he heard no second shot to get a fix on, he left the horse tied to a low limb and went ahead on foot. A man on a horse made as good a target as bushwhackers needed. A man afoot among huge old softwood trees offered poorer sightings.

An abrupt blizzard of gunfire erupted. It drove Jawn Henry to the far side of an enormous pine tree. This time there was no mistaking the direction of the gunfire — north a short distance and west.

For almost a full minute it sounded like a genuine war before silence fell; acrid-scented burnt powder spread ghost-like among the trees. Jawn Henry thought he heard voices. He must have been mistaken, but one thing he did hear and could readily identify was the whispery sound of a solitary horse coming toward him among the trees.

When the animal came into sight

about half of its panic had atrophied. In fact when Jawn Henry stepped forth to block the way, the animal halted stone-still, almost as though he welcomed the two-legged creature.

There was blood on the animal's left shoulder which Jawn Henry examined closely before deciding the blood was not the result of the animal being injured. There was also blood on the *rosadero* with a streak on the saddle-seat.

Jawn Henry loosened the cinch, tied the animal, appropriated someone's Winchester from the saddle-boot and resumed his hike in the direction of the gunfight.

He heard someone coming. Whoever he was, he had to be either agitated or foolish because he made as much noise as a cub bear chasing its tail.

Jawn Henry took position beside a huge, overripe old forest mammoth and waited while holding the appropriated saddle-gun low in both hands.

As the hastening man came closer

Jawn Henry eased back the dog of the Winchester. When the man came into sight Jawn Henry recognized him as a Cotswol rider without being able to recollect the man's name — if he'd ever heard it.

He waited. The rangeman was sweating hard, his mouth was open to suck air. To Jawn Henry he had all the indications of someone in shock.

Jawn Henry let the cowboy get almost up to his tree before stepping around it. The rangeman caught movement and spun with a clawed right hand flashing toward his hip-holster. Jawn Henry quietly said, "Leave it be! Take that hand away from the gun! *Do it, damn you!*"

The cowboy froze, wild-eyed and ashen. If he recognized the town constable he gave no such indication. He was young, possibly not quite twenty, lean and rawboned. Jawn Henry thought he should recognize the man but he didn't.

"Lift it out," he told the cowboy,

"with two fingers an' let it drop."

As the rangeman moved to disarm himself his eyes focused. He recognized the constable finally.

As he dropped the gun he sagged. "Rode right into it, Mister Mulligan. Damn Raine anyway. Come right up through some rocks as big as a house . . . did he swerve away? No! Rode right up into them gawddamned rocks."

Jawn Henry told the man to sit with his back to a tree. The cowboy looked up. "A massacre, that's what it was. I'd still be up there with 'em 'ceptin' I was ridin' a colt. He spooked, danged near lost me off when he whirled . . . constable?"

Whiskey would have helped. Jawn Henry stood in front of the range-rider. "How many was there?" he asked.

The cowboy lowered his head and wagged it. "Seemed like an army. Hell, they was in them rocks on both sides." He raised his head. "I seen Mister Cotswol go off first."

Jawn Henry pulled up to his full

height, slowly turned, then faced the rider to say, "Get on the far side of the tree. Move, damn it!"

The rider hadn't heard horsemen coming, slowly, in the direction from which the surviving Cotswol rider had fled. Jawn Henry said, "Not a damned sound."

"They'll shoot you down like a — "

"Shut up. Not a sound. You hear me?"

The cowboy nodded, pressed closer to his tree and could not see Jawn Henry, who listened briefly, arrived at a correct conclusion, and faded among the trees. They were tracking the rangeman who had escaped.

They halted somewhere beyond the constable's sight. He distinctly heard a man say, "Let him go. By now he's halfway down out of here."

This remark brought a sharp reply. "We get 'em all. We got to."

A solitary rider came into Jawn Henry's view riding slack and watching the ground. He was a stranger. Jawn

Henry could have emptied his saddle but he didn't. Two other men appeared, passing in and out of forest gloom, spread out in a loose line of the kind men use when they're stalking, making a sweep.

The first of them was dark, swarthy, Mex-looking or perhaps Indian. He was leaning to one side reading tracks. The other two were yards to the rear. One of them spoke to the 'breed reading tracks. "Suppose we don't find him? He'll get down yonder an' stir up a hornet's nest."

The 'breed answered without looking up. "We'll get him, an' we got to do it before he gets out of here."

The third man dryly said, "Jericho, we'd do better to leave off up here, go somewhere else where the risk ain't as great . . . what the hell, gettin' clear is worth more'n runnin' some danged rangeman down an' cuttin' his throat, ain't it?"

The dark man did not reply, he was studying tracks right up until he was no more than two hundred feet from Jawn Henry's area of concealment. He twisted in the saddle to speak to the men following when Jawn Henry very slowly and carefully began to raise the Winchester. Jericho the 'breed Indian must have had an eye in the back of his head. He flung himself from the saddle as Jawn Henry fired.

It wasn't the riders that exploded, it was their horses. One rider got off a hand-gun shot — straight into the treetops. Jawn Henry shot this one through the brisket. He was dead before he struck the ground.

The 'breed hit the ground rolling. When he stopped he fired from the hip. Jawn Henry bounced off a tree and fell. The third rider's horse ran under a low limb, his rider went off backwards. His horse was momentarily between the 'breed and Jawn Henry. In seconds he was past. The 'breed was bringing his six-gun to bear when Jawn Henry fired from the ground. The 'breed yelped, fired wild and flinched.

Jawn Henry's slug had torn the man's shirt and raised a welt along his ribs. He lost his six-gun as he twisted from shock.

The cowboy behind the tree peeked around, groaned and got to his feet. "There's more," he told Jawn Henry, whose response was profane. "Take off your belt an' cinch it around my leg."

The cowboy looked around before kneeling with the belt in his hand. His face was ashen. As he tightened the belt to stop the flow of blood he said, "That one that got knocked off is comin' round."

Jawn Henry was silent until the belt had been sufficiently tightened to stop the bleeding. Afterwards he growled at the Cotswol rider. "Get that man's gun!"

The stunned outlaw did nothing to prevent being disarmed. He was not completely recovered from being knocked senseless but afterwards, sitting on the ground looking from the wounded lawman to the Cotswol rider who had the outlaw's own sidearm cocked and aimed, he groaned.

The silence which returned smelled of burnt gunpowder. Otherwise the area was deathly silent. The horses were gone, birds too, nor would they return for the balance of the day.

The horses probably would not go far; their perception of panic rarely lasted long.

Jawn Henry's leg ached more than it pained. His britches were red-soggy and torn. There were two surviving outlaws, the 'breed called Jericho and the man who had forgot to duck when his horse ran under a low limb. Their companion was as dead as a man could be.

The Cotswol rider dropped the appropriated six-gun into his holster, did not pick up his own gun; the appropriated weapon was better.

Jawn Henry addressed him. "Did you see Mister Cotswol an' the men he come up here with get killed?"

The cowboy started to nod and

then checked himself. "I seen Mister Cotswol go off an' I seen Lame go off. The others must've got killed too, but about then is when the horse run away with me."

"Go back," Jawn Henry said. "Maybe they wasn't all killed. Go back an' see."

The cowboy was hesitant. In his heart he was satisfied his employer among others had been killed in the bushwhack and he wasn't eager to go back up there.

Jawn Henry gestured with his belt-gun for the 'breed and the other outlaw to sit close together in front of a tree where he could keep track of them.

They obeyed. The 'breed gazed malevolently at Jawn Henry who glared back when he addressed the other Cotswol rider. "Wait a minute. You know these two?"

The cowboy nodded and pointed to the man who had got knocked senseless. "Him. Carl Maxwell."

Jawn Henry ignored Maxwell when

he said, "Get a-horseback, ride to town an' fetch back some fellers to pack us out of here."

"You don't look real good, constable."

"Is that a fact? I don't feel real good. Now get a horse and be on your way."

"You'll be all right?"

"No, I won't be all right, an' you standin' there lookin' like a sick calf don't make me feel no better. Get a horse and do what I told you."

"What about Mister Cotswol? You said for me to — "

"Gawddammit, ride for town. If Raine is dead the wait won't matter. *Get the hell on your way!*"

The younger man walked off as the man named Maxwell spoke to Jawn Henry. "You know that feller?"

Jawn Henry scooted until his back was to a tree before saying, "No."

"Well, I do, an' he don't have the sense Gawd give a goose."

"How much sense does he have to have to get to town an' back? Mister, if he's dumb he didn't ride under a limb." Jawn Henry's leg-wound was the kind that bled a lot but there were no broken bones. He considered the other two. Either one would cut his throat at the first opportunity. He addressed the dark man. "What's your name?"

"Jericho. What's yours?"

"Jawn Henry Mulligan — constable. Jericho, I most likely have a Wanted dodger on you at the jailhouse."

The dark man sneered. "You want to sell it?"

Jawn Henry ignored that remark. "You'n Maxwell and someone else robbed a stage north of town. I expect you're goin' to tell me that dead feller did it."

"I'm not goin' to tell you anything," the dark man replied.

Jawn Henry smiled without a shred of humour, cocked the appropriated Winchester and pointed it directly at the 'breed. "In that case you can't do me any good alive or dead, an' the way I feel right now . . . won't nobody hear the shot, Jericho."

Maxwell spoke quickly. "You can't do that, constable."

"Why can't I? We'll wait until that Cotswol rider is a few miles down-country. He won't hear it an' when he gets back with help . . . you two jumped me. I fired in self-defence."

Jericho's tongue made a darting circuit of his lips. He alternately looked at the cocked gun pointed at him and the face of the man above it. But it was Maxwell who spoke into the brief silence.

"Cold-blooded murder, constable. That won't set well with folks."

"Like Jericho said — what they don't know won't make 'em worry. Pardner, we got time — tell me about the stage robbery."

Before Maxwell could reply the dark man sneered as he said, "Tell him nothin', Carl. He ain't goin' to shoot anyone."

Jawn Henry shifted the gun-barrel toward Maxwell. "Don't believe him.

I'd as soon shoot you as spit. Tell me about the stage robbery."

Maxwell lacked the 'bottom' of Jericho. The Winchester was aimed squarely at him from less than twenty feet. "I stopped it, took what I could get an' sent it on its way."

"Alone?" Jawn Henry asked, and Maxwell nodded. "They said there was three guns, Maxwell. I found sign of two other fellers east of the road. Want to try the truth this time?"

"They was over there in case I run into trouble. They propped their saddle-guns in the rocks west of me."

Jawn Henry gazed sardonically at the dark man. "Is that the truth, Jericho?"

"Go to hell."

Jawn Henry returned his attention to the Cotswol rider. "We got plenty of time. Tell me why you stole that horse in Mex-town in broad daylight."

"I didn't steal him. He belonged to me. I turned him loose when we got down here. Some old beaner trapped him." Maxwell had no difficulty with this discussion. "I rode that horse four years, constable. He never made a fault, an' he can run a hole in the daylight. I owned him an' took him back. That's the truth of it. Ask Jericho; I been ridin' that horse a long time. Jericho . . . ?"

"Shut up, Carl. Your tongue's hinged in the middle an' flaps at both ends."

Maxwell subsided. Somewhere in the middle distance a cougar screamed. Jericho said, "Smells them fellers we shot. Constable, you bled a lot too, an' you can't run if the cat scents you."

Jawn Henry gave the dark man a withering look as he said, "He better be bullet-proof."

The cat did not scream again. Silence settled with the dark man watching Jawn Henry like a hawk. Folks who bled eventually got sleepy. Jericho was waiting for this to happen to the lawman.

Maxwell sagged against a tree. He had a headache and a lump indicating the cause of it. Constable Mulligan sweated, infrequent flashes of light-headedness came and went. He was thirsty. Across from him Jericho sat like a statue, motionless, silent and watchful.

Jawn Henry knew what was happening to him; he also knew about how long it would take that Cotswol rider to reach town, get help and start back. He gazed at Jericho with a dispassionate gaze. "If you move I'll kill you," he told the dark man, and got a sneer in response. Jawn Henry shifted the Winchester back toward Maxwell. "Take off your belt. Tie his arms in front with it. Tie 'em hard."

Maxwell arose to obey and Jericho snarled at him. "Set down, Carl. He ain't goin' to shoot anyone."

Jawn Henry squeezed the trigger; the gun recoiled in his hands. The bullet struck the tree Maxwell had been sitting beside. He jumped. Jawn Henry levered up to fill the chamber and repeated it. "Tie his arms in front with your belt — real tight . . . the next one goes through your damn brisket. *Tie him!*"

Jericho looked past Maxwell as the rangeman knelt with his trouser-belt in hand. While Maxwell was lashing his arms at the wrists he did not look at Jericho, made a particular point of not looking at him.

When he had finished he remained crouching; Jawn Henry told him to go back to his tree and sit down. The highwayman arose as though to obey and turned with an under-and-over .44 calibre derringer in his right fist.

Jawn Henry squeezed the trigger again, this time braced for the recoil. Carl Maxwell squawked and dropped to both knees clasping his upper right arm.

Jericho swore a blue streak. The deringer was near his feet but with both arms secured he could not reach it.

Maxwell rolled on the ground grinding his teeth to keep from crying out. Blood soaked his shirt. Jawn Henry leaned against his tree waiting for the noise to abate. When it did he said, "You dumb son of a bitch. Take Jericho's belt and buckle it tight around your arm." He glared at the dark man. "Didn't have the guts to use it yourself, did you?"

Maxwell yanked the trouser-belt from the dark man and moaned as he lashed it around his arm. The bleeding stopped, all but an occasional trickle. Maxwell looked sick and probably felt sick.

Jericho's eyes, like those of a lidless rattler, never left Jawn Henry. While Maxwell was going back to his tree in a one-armed crawl Jericho coldly smiled at the constable. "Anyone with a lick of sense would go over someone for a gun. You ain't very smart, constable."

4

The Two Faces of Death

JAWN HENRY'S periods of light-headedness increased as the hours passed. That did not worry him as much as thirst did. Jericho had a red welt along his rib-cage. Maxwell was on the verge of being sick to his stomach from the shock of being wounded. There was a canteen on Jawn Henry's saddle but he could think of no way of getting it, so he alternately spit cotton and considered killing the 'breed, then crawling to the horse with Carl Maxwell in front.

That cougar screamed again, this time northward. It sounded closer to the boulders where the Cotswol riders had been ambushed. Jericho never once took his dark stare off the constable, but Carl Maxwell twisted around as though expecting to see the big cat.

Jawn Henry wondered about Maxwell. He wasn't acting like a hard-bitten renegade. Jericho interpreted the constable's gaze correctly. "Never had much guts," he said coldly.

Jawn Henry nodded about that. "You don't use good judgement in pickin' who you'll ride with," he told the 'breed.

Jericho was an individual who could not abide criticism, so his response was predictable. "An' you do? Ridin' up in here by yourself, gettin' yourself shot?"

Jawn Henry regarded the dark man through a long period of silence before speaking again. "How much did you gents get from the stage?"

"Go to hell."

Jawn Henry listened briefly to Maxwell's moaning before saying, "Shut up, you whinin' son of a bitch."

Maxwell did not make another sound.

Jericho examined his side where the angry swelling had increased. Jawn Henry said, "I'd give a year's wages to have a second chance."

Jericho squared around. "I'll give you a year's wages. How much do you make a month?"

"Not enough to let you two ride away, if that's what you're hintin' at."

Jericho got comfortable against a tree, stared unblinkingly at Jawn Henry. "You feelin' tired yet?"

"No. Not real happy but not tired."

"You will, you lost a sight of blood. You'll get real tired directly."

"If I do, Jericho, as soon as I feel real bad I'll kill you . . . where did you have that derringer?"

"Inside my pants in front. It was easy passin' it to Carl with his back to you, while he was facin' me up close."

"He was an idiot to take it."

"Well, no-one ever said Carl was right smart . . . constable?"

"What?"

"You got a price?"

"No."

"Everyone's got a price, constable."

"Jericho, the longer we set here the more I'm certain that I'm goin' to kill you."

Jericho smiled bleakly at the constable. "Killin' me ain't the problem, constable. Water is. You been lickin' your lips; you're thirsty. That's somethin' else I've learnt over the years. Men who've bled out a lot get thirsty."

"How many men you shot, Jericho?"

"Countin' In'ians an' Messicans — I don't know. Others like stupid posse-riders who ride into ambushes, I got no idea, but if I was to guess I'd say maybe upwards of fifty others. Emigrants I robbed on the trail, nighthawks ridin' herd in the horse-herds we needed."

"Why, Jericho?"

"I guess because they was there. Now it's my turn: where is your family?"

"I don't have a family."

"That's too bad, constable. A man should sow his seed if he wants to leave somethin' worthwhile behind."

64

"How about you, Jericho; you got a family?"

"In'ians, Messicans." The renegade briefly lost his malevolent glare. "I got wives . . . constable, settin' here waitin' for you to get puny so's I can kill you . . . you'n me ain't a whole lot different."

Jawn Henry snorted. The dark man flashed a dazzling smile. "You do what you get paid for. Me, I do what makes most men do anythin' at all. Make a living."

"Killin' and stealin'?"

"You know a better way for a 'breed to get money?"

"Did you ever try workin' for your money?"

"Yes, but not since I figured out there's more folks who don't like 'breeds than do, an' even the ones who don't care about the colour of your eyes don't pay the same as they do the other ones."

Maxwell got unsteadily to his feet. The 'breed ignored this but Jawn Henry

65

didn't. "Set down!"

Maxwell remained standing. "I got to have water."

Jawn Henry regarded the younger man sardonically. "We all need water. There ain't any. Set down!"

"There's a canteen where the ambush took place, constable."

"An' you're goin' to hike up there, get the canteen an' come back here?"

Jericho interrupted the two-way conversation. "He'll fetch back the canteen, constable." The 'breed put a steady gaze upon Maxwell. Within moments Maxwell nodded. Neither of them addressed the other.

Jawn Henry repeated it. "Set down!"

Jericho eyed the lawman. "He'll bring back water."

"He won't never come back an' you know it . . . an' sure as hell there's a gun lyin' around up there."

Jericho gestured on the good side of his upper body. "Go on, Max. Bring back all the canteens you can carry."

But Maxwell did not move.

Jawn Henry shifted the saddle-gun to bear on Maxwell's belt-buckle. An exasperated 'breed exclaimed loudly that Maxwell would return. He would give his word about that.

The constable's response was menacing. "Set down, you son of a bitch! *Set*!"

Maxwell sat. Jawn Henry returned his attention to the 'breed. "Not a damned word out of you!"

Jericho considered the lawman, seemed about to argue, when a new sound came to them; this time it was noisy and judging from that, it was large. Jericho's mouth, open to speak, froze in silence. He half twisted to peer in the direction of the new sound, so did Maxwell and Jawn Henry; all three were outdoorsmen, they knew the kind of animal that was approaching. It was the only animal in timbered uplands which did not use stealth, because it did not have to. A bear.

The animal stopped somewhere southwest of the rigid men, but only temporarily, and that was a characteristic which settled doubts the men might have had. Bears had poor eyesight. When they were hunting food, if it did not move they commonly missed seeing it. Because of this they halted often to tilt sensitive noses and detect scents.

The noise resumed. Bears only went around obstacles they could not push through. This animal had little to delay it but it nevertheless powered its way over small trees in a straight line.

When it halted the last time before the men saw it, the animal raised its head to make a part-whine, part-snarl. If there had been doubt before about this creature there was none after it growled.

Jericho spoke without looking at Jawn Henry. "It's comin' from downhill an' somewhat west of us. Constable — "

"Shut up," Jawn Henry said. "Shut up an' keep still."

The bear was on a scent but it was not hurrying. They heard it tear small trees out of its path. It also scored the bark off other trees in order to use its tongue in catching larvae, bugs, anything it could eat.

Maxwell was near to fainting. He hoarsely told the constable he wanted to go after one of the discarded weapons. Jawn Henry did not reply, Jericho did. "You stay here, Carl. It'd grab you before you could find a weapon."

Maxwell sank down against his tree and babied his wounded arm. Throwing caution to the wind he loudly proclaimed it was the lawman's duty to save Maxwell and Jericho if the bear moved into sight.

Jawn Henry regarded Carl Maxwell with disgust, shook his head and repeated something to Jericho he had said earlier.

The bear was less than two hundred feet from the waiting men when it came from behind a huge old bristle-top pine, reared up turning its head from side to side until it was satisfied in which direction it should go, then dropped down to all fours and stood there rocking back and forth.

Carl Maxwell had a good sighting of the bear — and fainted. Jericho quietly asked if Jawn Henry had a good view of the animal. Jawn Henry did not reply. He was as silent and rooted as a tree; every muscle and nerve in his body was concentrating on the bear.

It was an old boar bear, scarred from battles and probably with even worse vision than most bears had. He stood on all fours turning his head occasionally then repeating the routine over again.

Jericho, still sitting twisted, spoke to Jawn Henry from his vantage-place. "How many slugs left in that carbine?"

Jawn Henry did not reply. He was watching the bear, and right at the moment all he needed was one bullet, at the most two. He had no idea how many cartridges remained in the Winchester but was certain it had to be more than two.

Jericho faced back. "Check the

loads," he said, making it sound like an order.

Jawn Henry had a good view of the bear. It was a large, scarred, massive critter, and it was old. With an even chance he could kill the bear. Jawn Henry was deadly with both a long-gun and a sidearm. Up until now he had been anyway, but, while those feelings of light-headedness had not recurred lately, they could do so at any moment, and if one of them arrived now, the Winchester wasn't going to be enough unless he shot the old boar on a downward slant in the head, or straight through his heart aiming at his chest before things got blurry.

Bears did not ordinarily attack people, they fled from them, but old bears, unable to hunt successfully because of age-related impairment, would and did attack people. A large old bear required a lot of food and while it would gorge on wild berries and some plants when they were in season, a bear was first and foremost a meat-eater.

Every rangeman whose livelihood required combing uplands to drift cattle back to grassland had encountered bears whose choice of red meat was cattle when they were available. Despite size, heft and awkward appearance a bear could catch cattle providing he could get close before charging. A bear's speed was surprisingly fast for so ungainly an animal.

Jericho hoarsely whispered, "Shoot! What'n hell you waitin' for? Kill the son of a bitch."

The bear heard those words, halted to stand erect, swinging its head from side to side, peering from weak eyes. Jawn Henry was awed; standing on his hind legs the old boar was close to seven feet tall.

Jericho was sweating hard. If the old boar charged Jericho would be the first two-legged creature he would reach. "Shoot, you damned idiot," he cried out.

Jawn Henry raised the carbine as the bear dropped back down on all fours and hung there peering ahead, wrinkling its nose, making its decision.

Jericho gathered himself for a run. Jawn Henry said, "Keep still. You're in my way. Lie flat."

Jericho did not get down; he and the huge old bear watched each other. Jericho was like a coiled spring. Jawn Henry repeated it. "Get flat down. You're between me'n him."

The bear resumed his stalk, swaying, making his pigeon-toed walk without haste. He had seen enough movement to have a target.

Jawn Henry got the Winchester to his shoulder before feeling the peculiar, painless but incapacitating sensation of light-headedness coming.

He snugged the butt-plate into the curve of his shoulder, lowered his eye to the buckhorn sights, and saw not a bear but a massive blur that was approaching with a relentless but ungainly stalk.

To kill a bear required at least one bullet in a vital area. Just shooting a bear would not necessarily put him down. Jawn Henry lowered the Winchester, rubbed his eyes and raised it again. Now, his vision was clearer; not as clear as it normally was but clear enough to see the chest of the oncoming bear.

He said, "Steady, Jericho," and pulled the trigger. The bear was punched back onto its haunches. Jawn Henry levered up the next bullet and watched. With no idea how hard hit the old bear was, he watched and waited.

Not hard enough, evidently, because the bear got back onto all fours and growled, slobbered and resumed his seemingly unstoppable advance.

Carl Maxwell, probably roused by the gunshot, pushed himself off the ground, saw the oncoming bear and made a small frightened squawk before getting behind the nearest big tree.

This noise distracted the bear but he did not change the direction of his approach. This time Jericho sprang up, cursing the constable and screaming for him to shoot. He did all this while standing between the bear and the wounded lawman who was farther away with his back to a tree.

Jawn Henry paused long enough to drag a soiled cuff across his upper face. As before, this stratagem worked; within moments his vision was as nearly perfect as it had ever been. He raised the Winchester for his second shot. Sometime between the first and second hoistings of the weapon it had become very heavy.

Jericho ran, not only frantically but wildly. The old boar heard and watched, standing solidly on its massive legs. For the first time Jawn Henry had a clear sighting. He got the saddle-gun to his shoulder, blinked several times, whistled loudly so the bear would rear up again, and when it did Jawn Henry shot the bear through the heart. It didn't fall as much as it very abruptly folded into itself and went down in a great sprawl.

Carl Maxwell peeked around the base of his tree, saw the dead animal and slowly lowered his face to his arms and did not move until Jawn Henry called to him.

"Maxwell! Get up!"

The outlaw came up onto all fours looking over where the huge old boar-bear was sprawled-dead. He got unsteadily to his feet, approached Jawn Henry and sank down. "Good shootin'," he said in a husky voice. "That was one hell of a big 'un."

"Get behind me, put your back to mine, and don't move."

Maxwell obeyed. When they were back to back he said, "You figure Jericho won't shoot through me to get you, you're mistaken. If he wants you dead, constable, you could have three, four more fellers settin' in front of me — his old friends, in fact — an' he'd still kill you."

Jawn Henry scarcely heard, he was struggling to put off an oncoming dizzy spell and was failing. As moments passed he could sense himself slipping away into a world where nothing mattered, not even staying alive.

He could shoot Maxwell, who was a threat, but the real threat to Constable Mulligan was the 'breed Jericho, who had fled so fast that within moments he had become invisible among the forest giants.

Jawn Henry had to yield. He could not trust the cowboy and he had an idea, gathered from those murderous stares he had gotten from the 'breed, that Jericho would not go far, just far enough to wait and watch as he'd done before.

That he owed his life to the lawman would not mean the same thing to the 'breed outlaw it meant to other people.

He was out there; sooner or later he would acquire a weapon, come back and try one more time to kill the constable.

5

Hard Men

THE constable's pressure against the rangeman's back slackened. Maxwell risked twisting around. Jawn Henry had passed out, the Winchester lay slack across his lap. Maxwell very gently eased it away. The farther he moved the more the constable sagged, until he fell suddenly where Maxwell had been sitting.

The rangeman arose, leaned over, picked up the carbine, stuck the belt-gun in his pants top, stood a moment gazing at the unconscious lawman, turned to look elsewhere, saw the dead bear, saw trees and beyond them westerly a clearing where sunlight shone.

A hissing sound brought Maxwell around crouched, carbine cocked and ready. Jericho told Maxwell to point his weapon in some other direction. When the cowboy obeyed Jericho came from behind a forest giant. He asked if the lawman was unconscious. Maxwell nodded.

Jericho came closer, considered the lawman, made a little clucking sound and said, "Shoot him.

"I'll go find a pair of horses." He'd got out of the belt on his wrists, had it round his pants waist.

Jericho moved swiftly. Carl Maxwell watched him get lost among big old trees and turned back to owlishly regard the unconscious man. He raised and lowered the Winchester twice, finally turned away to seek Jericho and help him catch two horses.

Constable Mulligan opened his eyes, saw Maxwell walking westward with Jawn Henry's saddle-gun, and waited until Maxwell was well along in the direction of the clearing, then pushed upright, got the little under-and-over belly-gun, settled against a tree and came close to praying he wouldn't pass out again when the outlaws came back leading horses. Derringers only had two barrels, one above the other. They weren't worth much at a distance but up close they could drop a man.

The thirst became increasingly troublesome. Jawn Henry's wounded leg was swelling, each time he slackened the belt to allow blood to pass there was a trickle from the wound, but, surprisingly, the bleeding was much less than it had been.

Out of nowhere a blanket-wrapped canteen sailed close. Jawn Henry peered northward, saw no-one and reached for the canteen. He drank enough — not all he wanted but enough — put the canteen aside and turned his head.

Raine Cotswol was leaning against a tree, covered with drying dark blood. He looked like the wrath of God. Jawn Henry said, "Thanks. My tongue was gettin' thick."

The cowman looked carefully in all directions before sinking down to the base of his tree and speaking. "I'm the only one left. They was in some rocks . . . shot us up real bad. My shell-belt saved me but the slug swung me half around and off the horse. You look like hell."

Jawn Henry agreed. "An' I feel like hell."

"Where are the others?"

"I came up here alone."

Cotswol pointed. "Who is that one?"

"One of them. He got shot first off. You better sprout a third eye if you're goin' to stay here. Might be a good idea if you found some horses."

"You got bullets for that belly-gun?"

"Just the loads is all."

Cotswol arose, sashayed until he found a pair of six-guns which he presented to the constable with a crooked little smile.

Jawn Henry told the cowman about sending for help. Cotswol became pensive. "How long ago?"

"I sort of lost track of time. Three, four hours ago."

"That leg looks like hell."

"It feels like hell. Raine? Did they get all your riders?"

"Yes. Two died while I was workin' to save 'em. That's where I got bloody."

Jawn Henry said, "There's two of 'em, a 'breed named Jericho an' Carl Maxwell. They're lookin' for horses too. Be real careful."

The rugged older man's eyes narrowed.

"Maxwell?"

"Yes."

"I'll shoot that son of a bitch on sight."

Jawn Henry nodded. "Horses, Raine."

The cowman hesitated, saw the dead bear, wagged his head and walked out of sight among the trees. Jawn Henry drank, belched, drank more, stoppered the canteen and settled back. Sweat jumped out all over his hide. He examined the weapons, found them loaded and wondered what would happen next. Raine Cotswol was an old hand, he doubted that Jericho and Maxwell would see him before he saw them, and hoped very hard this would be the case.

They probably had no idea anyone had lived through their ambush. That, more than anything, would be in Raine's favour.

It was warm. Jawn Henry could not locate the position of the sun through treetops. Time actually did not matter except in the context of help arriving.

He was dozing when he heard horses. Raine was leading two, both saddled and bridled. Jawn Henry, half expecting it to be Jericho and Maxwell, had a cocked six-gun aimed when Raine appeared among the trees. As he tied the animals he said, "Didn't see hide nor hair of anyone. You sure they'd come back here?"

Jawn Henry wasn't sure but he had expected the 'breed to return. "I figured they might."

"Can you stand up?"

Jawn Henry wasn't sure about that

either. He had to loosen the belt before trying. Raine helped him. Jawn Henry felt giddy and leaned on his tree. "Give me a couple of minutes," he muttered, and concentrated on remaining upright until the period of light-headedness passed.

Loosening the belt for blood to flow made his toes tingle. Raine led a horse close to the tree, helped the constable get astride, then said, "Hold to the apple. If you pass out I'll try'n catch you."

Jawn Henry gripped the horn with his right hand, reins in his left hand. The two horses moved almost in unison, one behind the other. Raine rode twisted so he could watch Jawn Henry, who seemed to be doing well enough.

As they looked at one another the older man said, "I'd guess they found horses an' never looked back. Their kind don't settle in very well."

Jawn Henry accepted that, but remained watchful. Jericho and Carl Maxwell could be anywhere in the timber. Except for the fact that by now Jericho would recognize the need for quitting the country — maybe — Jawn Henry knew for a fact men like Jericho would not go far. Jericho had a murder to commit — Jawn Henry's murder.

The leg ached more than it pained; when Jawn Henry eased up the belt, there was blood. He hadn't expected anything else; a horse going downhill was not altogether different from a jack-hammer — less noisy but just as stiff-legged.

Jawn Henry drank again from the canteen. Except for the leg, he felt adequate — drawn out, tired all the way through, but adequate.

They did not talk on the down-slope ride. Raine kept his head moving, although after a few miles he felt reassured about the constable.

Between them they looked like they'd been butchering hogs; dried blood made their clothing stiff, they were filthy and haggard. They kept going on nothing less than 'bottom'. Fortunately both had plenty of that.

The sun was moving, there were shadows by the time they reached flat country. They had miles ahead of them before reaching Stillwater.

Although Jawn Henry was holding up well the cowman deviated slightly from their direct route, reached a creek with huge old shaggy cottonwoods bordering it on both sides, swung off and without a word went back to help the constable alight.

Jawn Henry had been riding a long time, the leg looked like an elongated balloon. Whatever its discomfort he had become inured to it right up until he allowed Cotswol to help him down, then he collapsed.

Jawn Henry cursed. Raine Cotswol knelt, examined the wound, loosened the belt a little, rocked back on his heels and shook his head.

He doused Jawn Henry with creek-water, mopped off some dried blood with swathes of grass, hunkered to roll and light a smoke which he offered to the constable. Jawn Henry shook his head. They spent a half-hour beside the creek, their animals dragging reins as they grazed.

About the time Cotswol thought it was time to get astride, both men heard riders easterly maybe a half-mile. It was difficult by waning daylight to see horsemen but the sound was unmistakable.

Raine said, "Goin' the wrong way."

Jawn Henry's reply was dry. "They didn't come from town, they're goin' toward it . . . Raine; you reckon that'd be Jericho an' your rangeman?"

Cotswol did not answer until the riders had passed far enough southward not to be heard, then all he said was, "If I was sure of that I'd leave you here for a spell."

When they resumed their ride Raine deliberately held to a westerly course which would eventually take them to the town, but not down the main thoroughfare. Jawn Henry said nothing but he was satisfied Cotswol was leery of those riders who had been riding over the tracks of the cowman and his companion.

An hour later, with town lights visible, Raine halted again, sat like a brooding bird, both hands atop the saddle-horn studying as much as they could make out in the dusk-light of Stillwater.

Jawn Henry said, "It didn't have to be them two. It could be anyone; riders from a ranch."

Old Cotswol sat gloweringly silent for a long time before saying, "Mebbe you're right, an' mebbe you ain't, but I'll tell you one thing, partner, if it was them two, we're not in shape to face 'em; and if it's them they could hang around town until we got there. From what I know, them two is real good at back-shootin'."

Cotswol resumed the ride, roughly a quarter-mile west of the lights, reached the lower end of Stillwater, passed well below before turning eastward, crossing the road and heading for Mex-town.

The only thing he said as he did this was, "Can't be too careful, Jawn Henry. You ain't fit an' I don't feel fit neither."

They stopped beside the large *jacal* of Sixto Erro, one of the few residences that showed light.

Again, the cowman helped the lawman get down, only this time before Jawn Henry's legs gave out Cotswol got him settled on an old bench before going back to care for their animals.

Someone appeared in a rear doorway holding a lantern. Jawn Henry said, "Elena, it's me, the constable."

"Who is that putting horses in the corral?" she asked.

"Raine Cotswol. We been shot up."

She held the lantern higher and gasped. When Raine returned she told him to get on one side of Jawn Henry while she got on the other side. This way they got him inside, steered him to a bedroom and eased him down atop the bed. Through clenched teeth the lawman said, "Whiskey!"

Sixto's wife handed Cotswol the bottle in the doorway and fled, head covered with a shawl. Somewhere in the house the cowman and constable could hear a man's deep, resonant snoring, which was reassuring to Jawn Henry; it meant Sixto was recovering.

Elena Erro returned in the company of a heavy, very dark woman whose head was also covered by a shawl. In feeble lantern-light she looked no more than twenty — in fact she was in her late fifties, her name was Carman Rosa, she was Mex-town's *curandera*.

Elena left her with the haggard men. She asked if Cotswol was injured. He shook his head and pointed toward Jawn Henry.

The *curandera* went to the bedside, poked the swollen leg, leaned to sniff, then left the room and returned with an old satchel from which she removed a number of articles as she explained what she intended to do, and having told Cotswol what she expected of him, she clamped a strong-smelling cloth over Jawn Henry's face.

When he awakened the moon was far down, the room was cold, there was a candle burning on a small table, Raine was sprawled asleep in a rickety old chair, and there was no sign of the *curandera*.

The wounded leg only hurt now when he moved it, which he avoided doing. His face itched, he was thirsty and had been covered during the night so he was comfortably warm.

He scented wood-smoke, Mex-town was awakening to a new day. He was as helpless as a kitten. If Jericho knew where he was there was no way he could defend himself, his weapon had been taken away sometime in the night. Cotswol's ruined shell-belt still had a full holster but he was sleeping like the dead and Jawn Henry could not reach him.

Elena Erro appeared in the doorway; they exchanged a look and she disappeared without a word. Not much later she returned with two thick crockery mugs full of hot black coffee. She had to roust Raine three times before he was really awake.

Jawn Henry asked about her husband. She put a soulful, black-eyed look on him as she said, "He is doing well. That priest who visits once a month came by, blessed Sixto and prayed. Right after he left my husband smiled for the first time and wanted me to get into bed beside him."

Raine left to visit the emporium to buy new clothing and to use the barber's wash-house out back for an all-over bath.

He did not return for several hours. Added to the list of things he intended to do was get a shave and get information about the riders who had ridden to the uplands from town.

When he got back to the *jacal* the hefty *curandera* was working on Jawn Henry while Elena Erro watched from the doorway. When Raine would have barged in Elena Erro scowled and shook her head at him. "The doctor

92

does not like people looking over her shoulder."

The hefty woman gave Cotswol a sulphurous glare and turned back to her work.

Raine went looking for Sixto Erro, found him comfortably propped up and pulled a stool to bedside. Before he could ask how the larger man was feeling Sixto said, "Jawn Henry talked in his sleep. He said you'n your riders was ambushed. Did that happen?"

Raine nodded without speaking. Right now and for the rest of his life he would not discuss what happened in the uplands. But he told Sixto what else had happened and the large man made a clucking sound. "If they came here to finish what they started, where are they?"

"I got no idea, but I can tell you they didn't show up at the hotel nor bed down in the hay at the livery-barn."

"Maybe, then, they didn't come here, eh?"

Raine shrugged. "Maybe, but I

wouldn't bet a plugged *centavo* on it. One's some kind of 'breed the other's that rider of mine that took the horse from down here, Carl Maxwell."

"An' your other riders?"

"We was ambushed. That's all I got to say. I come through, the others didn't."

Sixto's black gaze was fixed on Cotswol. "How did Jawn Henry get shot?"

Cotswol stood up, expressionless and bitter-eyed. "He can tell you in a few days. You need anythin'?"

"Yes. A new body."

Raine returned to the other doorway where the *curandera* was wiping her hands and arms while she and Sixto's wife talked in Spanish. They stopped the moment the cowman appeared. The *curandera* gathered her things, would not meet Cotswol's gaze and departed.

Elena Erro went to Jawn Henry's bedside. On a small table nearby was a dead chicken. She put a cool palm on Jawn Henry's forehead and tiredly smiled. "You will be fine. There was no infection, though, only God knows why not, you and your clothing were filthy."

When she too departed she would not meet the cowman's gaze. Jawn Henry considered the older man in the doorway. "Moccasin telegraph. The whole town knows what happened up yonder. Don't ask me how, but they know. An' they know I'm here at the Erro house."

This last sentence was delivered dryly. Cotswol went to a bedside stool and sat down. He told the constable he looked better than Cotswol felt. He also told him six men from town had gone north with the messenger Jawn Henry had sent for help.

Jawn Henry was unmoved by everything the cowman said. He had been fed, washed and bandaged properly. As long as he remained absolutely still there was no pain, but the slightest movement brought it swiftly.

"Where are they?" he asked, and Cotswol gave his head a slight wag.

"I got no idea. I asked around. Only a few folk, like the mercantile owner, the liveryman an' the feller who minds the saloon on holidays. None of them know who Jericho is, nor Maxwell either for that matter." Cotswol rallied briefly. "They're gone, Jawn Henry. Most likely across the Mex border by dawn this morning." As he finished speaking Raine jutted his jaw in the direction of the little nearby table. "Did they feed you raw chicken?"

"No. The Mex lady-doctor busted the chicken down the middle an' tied it on my wound. She said it'd draw the poison out."

Cotswol looked dubiously at the dead chicken. "They got their ways, we got ours. What'n hell can a dead chicken do for a wound?"

"All I know is that she told me it'd

draw out any poison. It's hard on chickens but if it works . . . Raine, I don't like lyin' here waitin' for that son of a bitch."

"You got a gun?"

"Yes. Sixto's woman gave me one. It's under the pillow. But if they know where I am . . . that 'breed's no fool. I don't like bein' a sittin' duck. I'd feel better if I was in the jailhouse. There's only one door over there."

Cotswol arose. "I'll see about gettin' some fellers to carry you over there."

Jawn Henry spoke quickly. "Get 'em from Mex-town. By now I expect everyone in Gringo-town knows all anyone'd have to know to have some bastard volunteer to carry me over yonder, and blow my head off on the way."

Raine Cotswol didn't agree with such a precaution. It showed on his face. But he nodded. "I'll round 'em up," he told the constable and departed.

Elena Erro came to the doorway. "Do you feel better?" she asked.

Jawn Henry nodded. "As long as I lie still."

"Are you hungry?"

"I don't like bein' a burden."

The woman answered without any expression. "All men are burdens to all women. Are you hungry?"

"Yes'm."

She turned away. Jawn Henry thought about what she had said. He had never thought about it, but now he did, and the more he pondered the more inclined he was to believe she was probably right. For a fact he was a burden and so was her husband.

The house was cool. All adobe houses with mud walls three feet thick were cool in summertime. Nor were they hard to heat during cold weather. There was a large crucifix above the bed where Jawn Henry lay, the beads as large as the first joint of a man's thumb. The cross and its carving were crude but expressive.

Most of the residences in Mex-town had something equal, or even larger and more elaborate, in some room. Above the bed it invited God's intervention to protect people from harm, from the wily, malicious torment of *Señor Satan*.

Jawn Henry slept until Sixto's woman brought food. He ate every crumb. She had taken the tray away when Raine Cotswol arrived with four husky Mexicans and a stretcher made from two knotty poles and an old army blanket. As the Mexicans entered the room with the stretcher each man crossed himself. That massive old rosary was intimidating.

Elena came to watch Jawn Henry grind his teeth as he was lifted to the stretcher. She brought a sheet, covered Jawn Henry from head to toe, then held the door for the stretcher-bearers to leave. Raine turned, smiled, and handed Elena Sixto a small buckskin pouch. When she would have protested he said in Spanish, "For the church if you wish, but it is not payment because your kind of hospitality cannot be valued. It is from the heart. You are a lady. Goodbye."

Under the sheet Jawn Henry was surprised; he'd had no idea the old cowman spoke Spanish, nor any idea the rough, gruff old stockman knew anything about gallantry.

6

John Barleycorn at Work

IT was unavoidable that as soon as the stretcher-bearers crossed into Gringo-town people saw the completely shrouded body they were carrying, and immediately gossip blossomed up and down both sides of Gringo-town's main thoroughfare.

Constable Mulligan was dead!

A couple of crusty old tobacco-chewers out front of the saloon watched as the stretcher was carried into the jailhouse and one of them said, "It don't have to be Jawn Henry, does it? That sheet could cover a small horse."

But the prevailing snap-judgement, like most of its kind, was accepted and eventually enlarged upon. The only question which did not lend itself to an early resolution was why the dead man had been carried to the jailhouse instead of down to the carpenter's shop where coffins were made for three dollars each, and from where most funeral processions originated.

Because Raine Cotswol accompanied the stretcher-bearers and afterward went over to the cafe to eat, he was descended upon by townsmen with questions, none of which he answered. In fact he seemed deaf, ate without haste, paid the cafeman and shoved through the crowd, crossed to the jailhouse, barred the door from the inside and told Jawn Henry he was thought to be dead. Jawn Henry didn't laugh but the rugged old cowman did.

Later, when Father Ruiz came over to the jailhouse and was allowed inside, dozens of eyes saw this and were more than ever convinced the constable was dead. Father Ruiz had a following in Gringo-town, but his largest congregations were from Mex-town. Predictably, the devout put their own interpretation on the priest's visit — the giving of last rites.

Cotswol and the priest were amused. Jawn Henry would have been too if he hadn't felt like something a pup would drag from a tan-yard.

They got whiskey down him, which helped, but his greatest problem was thirst. They left a canteen on the side of the jailhouse bunk where Jawn Henry was bedded down. He drank, dozed off, awakened, drank more water and dozed off again. After the second time several townsmen banged on the door demanding to know what had happened and how their town marshal had been killed.

Initially Father Ruiz may not have suspected anything, but those two old tobacco-chewers did more than suspect — they downright didn't believe the local lawman was dead.

What none of them had anticipated was the fierce backlash in Gringo-town to the fact that Jawn Henry had been killed, or perhaps had died the previous night from complications arising from a fight with outlaws.

This attitude set off a fire-storm of searches. The town was gone through several times and although a few outlanders were around, taken as a whole the locals' handling of things created the kind of loud-mouthed confusion which could be exploited by those likely to benefit.

With trouble brewing, as many outlanders as could left town. Mostly, they were travelling peddlers who never stayed long anyway. All this happened between the time the stretcher was carried into the jailhouse and sunset of the same day.

The agitation was increased when the riders who had gone up-country returned with dead men across their horses, something Raine Cotswol missed seeing because he had gone north to bring back his dead rangemen and missed seeing the townsmen doing the same thing; and for some bizarre reason it was thought Cotswol's disappearance from town had a dark side to it — why hadn't the cowman waited to witness the arrival of his dead riders?

Elena Erro came to the jailhouse after dark accompanied by the *curandera*. A Mexican who admitted them closed and barred the door afterwards, a questionable precaution because the saloon was now headquarters for angry and troubled townsmen who could agree on just one thing — someone deserved to be hanged.

Jawn Henry, with no idea of the extent of Stillwater's turmoil, but aware that something was going on, got little information from Sixto's wife and none at all from the *curandera*. She was at the jailhouse for just one purpose. This time when she removed the bandaging, her face brightened. There was no tell-tale edge of redness.

She told Sixto's wife in Spanish it was the will of God. If Sixto had been there, or if Jawn Henry had understood Spanish, they might have said the dead chicken deserved equal credit.

The *curandera* cleaned the wound, disinfected it again with a concoction that stung when applied and smelled as though spoiled eggs were part of the ingredients. Jawn Henry looked stoical but really wasn't. He asked Sixto's wife how her husband was. She replied with eyes rolled heavenward. "He won't stay in bed."

The *curandera*, bending to her work, said one word about Sixto Erro. *"Estupido."*

Someone rattled the barred roadway door with a heavy fist. The Mexican in the office came swiftly to the cell looking worried. Jawn Henry told him to ask who it was. His expression did not change so Elena Erro returned to the office with him. The Mexican could not speak English.

She called to the person outside. "Who is it?"

The answer was terse. "I got a message for the constable."

Sixto's wife spoke in Spanish. "Your name is what?"

Whoever was out there was quiet so long it began to appear he had departed. Then he rattled the door again. "Talk American," he exclaimed, and hit the door with his fist.

Sixto's woman tried again. "What is your name?"

"What is it you want?"

"My name ain't important. I got to see the constable."

Elena Erro looked at the uncomprehending Mexican and shrugged. "Don't open the door," she told him in Spanish, and was walking across the office when the man outside rattled the door and called out at the same time.

"We got a doctor for the constable. Let us in."

This time Sixto's wife gave an answer that was carried to the saloon. She said, "He doesn't need a doctor." What she meant was that the *curandera* was with Jawn Henry. What the man outside thought she meant was that Jawn Henry no longer needed a doctor because he was dead.

When the *curandera* had finished, was lowering her sleeves, she looked steadily at the constable. Her English was much better than her disposition. It should have been, she had been raised in a Catholic orphanage.

"I don't know why you aren't infected. How often do you take a bath?"

Jawn Henry reddened. "As often as I need one. How does the leg look?"

"It looks fine. I think you heal fast. But it takes longer for the blood to build up again. You should stay in bed, for two weeks eat lots of meat. After that," the woman shrugged. "After that a little walking, a little riding, no lifting, no drinking, go often and sit in the sun." She finished with her sleeves, gathered her belongings and went as far as the cell door before also saying, "Do you know the people in Gringo-town think you are dead? They saw a body covered by a sheet brought here."

The *curandera* smiled, not warmly,

sardonically. "By all rights you should be."

In the front office where she met Elena Erro the *curandera* sighed and rolled her eyes. "Men! That one back there should be dead."

Elena Erro smiled tiredly. "Please go see Sixto."

"I did before I came here. Do you know what the man was doing? Eating goat-cheese and drinking wine in your kitchen — him half dead only a few days ago. Men! *Estupidos!*"

The *curandera's* most relevant deed of the day occurred as she crossed from the jailhouse toward the dog-trot between buildings which was a common short-cut between Gringo-town and Mex-town. Two men waylaid her there. Both had been informed by watchers out front of the saloon of her entry to the jailhouse and her exit from it. Both smelled powerfully of liquor. One of the men was tall, thin, with a prominent adam's-apple and a false smile on his face when he barred the *curandera's* access to the dog-trot.

The other man was shorter. His hairline came to within three inches of his eyebrows. He did not smile. "You been at the jailhouse," this man said, speaking harshly. "Why? What you doin' over there?"

The *curandera* was not a person to be easily intimidated, under most conditions, but this time her accosters reeked of whiskey. She had been married twice, both times to men who drank and were abusive. She said, "I went to change the bandage on the constable."

The men stared. Eventually the tall one said, "That's a lie, folks don't put bandages on dead men."

The *curandera* looked steadily at the tall man. "He is not dead."

The shorter man became agitated. "Of course he's dead. You're lyin', woman. I got half a notion to break your — "

"Shut up," the tall man snarled. When his companion became silent, the tall man spoke quietly. "Constable Mulligan ain't dead?"

"No, he is not dead. He was shot in the leg. I was looking after the wound . . . get out of my way."

They yielded, watched the *curandera* make her way down through the dog-trot, then hastened back to the saloon to drop what amounted to a bombshell. It was greeted with a long silence. Eventually two old gaffers sitting near the stove looked down along the bar as one of them said, "They had him over in Mex-town an' fetched him back up here on a stretcher covered by a sheet, or something." The other man spat amber into the sandbox which surrounded the stove before he too spoke, sounding thoroughly disgusted.

"You herd of idiots. Who was you goin' to hang? I know that *curandera*. She wouldn't lie if you held her feet to a fire. If she says Jawn Henry's alive down there, then gawddammit he's alive down there."

One of the townsmen who had gone

111

up-country and had brought the dead Cotswol riders back to town raised his voice. "Let's go down there an' make certain."

Two men half-lost in the smoke of the saloon crowd exchanged a look. One of them the barman knew, not well but as an occasional customer. The other man, dark as a Mexican, the saloonman had never, to his knowledge, seen before.

The suggestion to go down to the jailhouse was favoured by some of the saloon's customers, but not all. The dissenters were not really doubtful after all they'd heard about Jawn Henry being dead. They simply were reluctant about going out into the chill of pre-dusk when remaining where they were was preferable.

About half of them were ready to march. They made an impressive picture backgrounded by a red, dying sun, striding purposefully in the direction of the jailhouse, some of them yawing a little as they hiked along, but all of them full of what they perceived as righteous resolve.

This time when someone beat on the jailhouse door, Sixto's wife ignored the agitated Mexican from the office. She told him short of using dynamite they'd never get inside. The Mexican paled under his normally ruddy complexion. He told her it sounded like many men outside. She returned to the cell where Jawn Henry asked what the commotion was about. When she told him he rolled his eyes without speaking.

The Mexican was reluctant about returning to the office so Sixto's wife accompanied him. The men outside were agitated about not being admitted. Sixto's wife waited for the profanity to slacken before she spoke. "What do you want?"

"To see Jawn Henry an' right damned now. Open the door or we'll blow it open."

Elena Erro gestured for the Mexican to raise the *tranca* which he hesitated about doing long enough to say, "There are many men out there. If you let them inside . . . they have been drinking."

The woman said, "Open it!"

As soon as the bar was lifted several men crowded in. Elena Erro faced them. When they would have pushed roughly past her to enter the cell-room she said, "Wait." She might as well have been talking to stones. They pushed her roughly aside. Behind them a man roared angrily. The last men to enter were abruptly seized by the clothing and hurled back outside. One man turned, saw the huge dark man coming, ducked away and fled out into the night. Three men were about to enter the cell-room when the commotion behind them made them look back. Sixto Erro grabbed one of the men who had roughly knocked his wife aside, lifted him bodily, twisted and hurled the man against a wall. He had meant to pitch him out the door. He missed. The man struck the wall, broke an old chair as he fell and lay sprawled.

The other two men were rigid. Sixto went for them with hands closed into claws. One man dropped low and fled before the big Mexican could grab him. The other man seemed to have taken root.

Sixto closed a fist around this man's shirt, pulled him close and cursed him in two languages. "Hit my wife, will you?" He lifted the man six inches off the floor, struck him twice in the soft parts and let him fall. The man sank to the floor like a broken doll.

Sixto was breathing hard. The jailhouse office was empty except for his wife who, in true womanly fashion, scolded her husband for not staying in bed at home.

He sank down on a bench, smiling. "The *curandera* told me. What did they want?"

"To see if Jawn Henry was alive."

"He is, isn't he?"

"Yes. Come along."

Sixto nearly filled the dingy little

corridor as he followed his wife. Jawn Henry was perched on the edge of the bed when they entered the cell. His eyes widened at sight of Elena's husband. Sixto gave him no chance to speak. He said, "They was drunk. They wanted to see you was alive."

Jawn Henry eyed the large man. "Bust down my jailhouse to find out?"

Sixto sat down on a little stool. He was winded, which made him shake his head. He had never before run out of energy so quickly. Elena pushed Jawn Henry back down, covered him and told her husband to come along. She left without another word except for the Mexican in the office who was sitting on a bench looking at the dark man Sixto had knocked senseless when he flung him against the wall. *"Estupido gringo!"*

Elena gazed at the unconscious man, stooped, freed the tie-down holding the stranger's six-gun in its holster, lifted the gun away and handed it to the Mexican. "When he comes around make him leave and throw his gun out after him."

The Mexican nodded and accepted the weapon, which was better than his, dropped his gun which did not always fire when it should, and holstered the better gun. He raised goats in Mex-town and was not by nature a violent man.

Elena and her husband used the same dog-trot to reach Mex-town the *curandera* had used, and they were seen doing it, but no-one offered to confront them for an excellent reason. Three of the saloonman's steadies had been hurt in the jailhouse, not seriously. Except for their pride they would be as good as new in a few days. One factor was clearly evident, they were stone-sober when they got back to the saloon.

One of the old gaffers who were sitting near the stove as they had been most of the evening, asked where the other two fellers were who had gone down yonder. No-one answered because no-one knew anything about those two men and right at this time did not care.

The barman set up drinks. There was no talk for a long time, but eventually a bruised individual near the lower end of the bar said, "We still don't know if he's alive or dead."

The man nearest him answered for all the others. "An' right now I don't give a damn."

One of those crusty old men near the stove picked up on the last man's remark. "He's alive; if you'd used your heads when you first heard about the Mex woman-healer bein' down there, you'd have known he was alive . . . *curanderas* don't have nothing to do with dead folks, only live ones."

That comment did not sit well with the battered patrons but no-one made an issue of it.

Eventually the patrons thinned out. When even the old gaffers were gone, the saloonman and two townsmen remained at the bar. One of the townsmen paid for a jolt, downed it, blew out an unsteady breath and spoke ruefully.

"Last I heard Sixto was down in bed."

The second townsman, with a swelling eye which was gradually becoming swollen and purple, gazed at his refilled glass without making any motion to raise it. He said, "What'n hell did we go down there for?"

His companion looked down his nose at the speaker. "To see if Jawn Henry was alive, what'd you think we went down there for?"

The second townsman did not answer the question, instead he said, "Well, old John Barleycorn sure set us up, didn't he? That big Messican was mad enough to chew spikes and spit rust."

"Sixto Erro," stated the saloonman. "He's a good hand. I never even heard of him gettin' mad before."

The man with the closing eye fixed the saloonman with his good eye. You should've been down there. He come in behind us. Someone must've jostled that Mex woman — his wife — he was like a wild bull." The speaker looked around and back. "There was two other fellers, one dark enough to be a Messican or a 'breed. The other feller — "

The saloonman interrupted. "He rides for Raine Cotswol. He's been in a few times. That's all I know about him."

"Them two didn't come back with the rest of us."

The saloonman shrugged. "Don't matter much. Most likely they rode out to the Cotswol place."

"If they was able to set a horse," a townsman said. "Sixto's stout as they come."

The saloonman agreed with that. "I've seen him lift a mustang pony on his shoulders. But for a fact I never saw him lose his temper."

The man with the puffy eye fixed the saloonman with the uninjured eye. "If you'd been along tonight you'd have seen him lose it. But no, the rest of us went down there but you had your bar to watch."

The saloonman became busy with a sour wet cloth wiping his bar.

7

A Very Near Thing

JAWN HENRY was testing himself with small movements. When they produced very little pain, he pushed himself harder.

He did not hear the man coming down from the office and did not see him until he was in the ajar cell doorway. They looked steadily at each other for a long moment before Jericho said, "Did you figure I'd forget, constable?"

Jawn Henry's answer was low. "No."

Jericho leaned in the doorway. He was in no hurry. He had developed a liking for seeing people sweat with fear. He was enjoying it now as he smiled.

"You stirred up the town. Folks thought you were dead. Well; I don't want to disappoint 'em."

Jawn Henry asked where Maxwell was. Jericho shrugged. "He don't matter. He never had the guts it takes, anyway. Constable, remember that talk we had back up yonder? Well, there was somethin' else I should've told you. Men ain't bad, circumstances make 'em bad."

Jawn Henry considered the distance between them. It would have been too great if he had been well and fit. As long as Jericho talked the better it would be, although Jawn Henry was enough of a realist not to expect a miracle.

He commented on Jericho's observation about men being bad. "Circumstances, maybe, but I can name ten men who had circumstances against 'em an' didn't go bad."

"Name me one, constable."

"Abe Lincoln."

"Another one."

"William Bent."

"Who's he?"

"It don't matter, but he built

forts and fair-traded with In'ians an' emigrants."

Jericho sucked his teeth for a moment before lifting out the Colt and tipping it upwards. "Are you a prayin' man, constable?" he asked.

"Not a real good one, Jericho. Seems since I was a button an' prayed I never got no answer. I guess a man could say he's taught to pray, but whether prayers are answered — seems to me they ain't."

Jericho allowed the gun muzzle to droop. "Constable, there ain't no such thing as prayers bein' answered most likely never was."

The gun muzzle steadied. Jericho smiled again. "I'll give it to you, constable, you don't scare worth a damn."

Jawn Henry gave an unhurried reply. "No such thing as a man who don't scare."

Jericho nodded slightly as he cocked the six-gun. The distance between them was less than fifteen feet. Jawn Henry bunched himself to roll off the cot. He was beginning to roll when Jericho pulled the trigger.

The gun did not fire. The audible sound of the hammer dropping was the only sound. Jawn Henry, ready to leave the bed, hesitated as he watched the dark man re-cock the gun as he cursed. This time Jawn Henry left the cot. When he landed on the floor all the pain he had thought had abated returned with breath-taking force.

Again the six-gun snapped without firing. Jericho held the gun up, staring at it. Jawn Henry was twisting to arise. Jericho re-cocked the gun for the third time and fired it. He didn't aim, at that distance he didn't have to, but Jawn Henry was moving. The gun fired, making a sound in the confinement of the cell like a cannon. The slug missed Jawn Henry by six inches, struck the rear wall, making a vertical crack.

Jawn Henry was upright when Jericho cocked the weapon again. Jawn Henry was moving toward him when Jericho squeezed the trigger. The gun misfired again. As Jawn Henry lunged, Jericho hurled the gun at him, jumped through the doorway and raced up the corridor to the office. Up there, he raised the *tranca* from its hangers, yanked open the door and disappeared in the night.

The one time the old gun had fired made echoing reverberations up through town. Even in the saloon men heard the sound. Several of them went to the spindle doors and peeked out. There was a light at the jailhouse. No-one was sure where the echoes had come from. All but two old men returned to their card-games or the bar.

The two old gaffers shuffled out into the night, muttered to each other, crossed the roadway and hiked as far south as the jailhouse. They did not seek entry, they did not even knock. Neither old man had a gun nor would have used it if they'd had guns. They hiked right on past, went down as far as the livery-barn and met the nighthawk standing out front craning up the roadway. The nighthawk said, "You gents hear a gunshot?"

They had. One old man said, "I never liked trouble that comes in the night. Come along, partner."

The night hostler went back down the runway to the harness-room where two candles were burning.

The pair of old men went to the extreme lower end of Stillwater where they shared a tar-paper shack.

Jawn Henry retrieved the six-gun Jericho had flung at him, sat down to remove the cylinder, cocked the weapon and squeezed the trigger. The firing-pin had been so worn that it only infrequently managed to strike the cap of a bullet.

Jawn Henry tossed the thing aside, started to stand up and all the torments of hell raced through his body. He made it back to the cot, but just barely.

Fifteen minutes later the *curandera*

arrived, mad as a wet hen. She pulled the blanket back, put both hands on ample hips and swore in Spanish. It was a good thing Jawn Henry did not understand.

Among all the things she called him, one was the ultimate insult.

"It is bleeding," she snarled. "Look what you've done." She exploded in Spanish again, giving Jawn Henry a further curse. "Go hit your mother!"

Behind her someone coughed in the doorway. It was the priest. The *curandera* leaned over Jawn Henry, cheeks red, mouth pulled into a slit.

Father Ruiz entered the cell. "I was close by. There was a gunshot from in here and a man ran out. What happened?"

"His gun misfired," Jawn Henry said.

"That's all?"

"Father, it's between him an' me."

The *curandera* exploded again. "That man can run. What can you do? Lie here like a lump of — "

The priest coughed again.

" — Like a lump of dung, then."

Father Ruiz settled on the three-legged stool. "Who is this man?" he asked.

"A renegade. Messican or 'breed, I don't know. His name is Jericho. It's a long story, father — Ow! What are you doing, woman?"

The *curandera* glared. "I'm closing what you tore open, *estupido*. Hold still. It will hurt. If you move I'll walk out of here and you can bleed to death. *Hold still*!"

Someone entered up front. The priest went to make an interception. It was a townsman; his name was Harkness, he was the saddle- and harness-maker. He wanted to know about the gunshot.

Father Ruiz lied with a clear conscience. "The constable was cleaning his gun. It accidentally went off."

"Can I see him, father?"

"Not now. Be patient. Maybe tomorrow."

"But father, the fellers at the saloon sent me to — "

"Maybe tomorrow. Go tell them it was an accident."

The harness-maker retreated grudgingly.

Father Ruiz closed and barred the door, returned to the cell-room where the *curandera* had found, and lighted, another lamp. This one hissed, its light was very bright.

She finished working on the injured leg, rolled down her sleeves and gazed disapprovingly at Jawn Henry, but her earlier fury had burned itself out. She addressed the priest in Spanish. "This one is fool out of fools. Why there is no blood-poisoning only God knows. If this imbecile breaks the wound open one more time I will not come. Goodnight, father."

At the door she looked back. This time she used English. "Every time you re-injure the leg means more weeks on your back." She then hurled another insult, in Spanish. *"Puerco hedor!"*

After the woman had gone Jawn Henry faced the priest. "What did she call me?"

"She did not call you anything . . . she said you smell like a pig." The priest also said, "She is the best we have. Don't make her angry."

"She was born angry," growled Jawn Henry. "That man you saw run out of the jailhouse — which way did he go?"

"Toward the livery-barn. Who was he?"

Jawn Henry ignored the question. "He'll be miles from here by now."

"What difference does it make? You can't go after him. He is gone, let it go at that."

"He'll be back, father."

Ruiz stood up. "I'll ask some men to come and sit with you."

"No. We'll settle this, just him an' me."

The priest seemed about to argue, closed his mouth, made the sign of the cross in the direction of the bed, and departed. There was no way for him to drop the *tranca* on the back of the door into place, but he made sure the

131

door was properly closed.

Whether the priest was responsible or not, Sixto Erro entered the jailhouse, noisily dropped the tranca into place from the inside and went down to Jawn Henry's cell.

Jawn Henry had heard someone enter. He was sitting up on the cot watching the door. When he saw Sixto he relaxed. The large Mexican grinned widely. "You was scairt, eh?"

"Maybe."

Sixto produced two guns, a Colt and a derringer. He put both on the bed. "Elena took the little gun from you when they brought you in." Sixto saw the worthless gun on the floor, stared at it a moment before picking it up and turning it in one large hand. "*Comita*," he said. "This old gun belongs to Arturo Melendez the goat-man." Sixto leaned over holding the butt-plate toward Jawn Henry. Crudely etched into steel were the initials A. M.

Jawn Henry explained about the gun.

How Jericho had got it he could not explain. Sixto sat on the little three-legged stool. The constable studied him. For a man who had been injured as badly as Sixto had been, he looked remarkably healthy. He asked if Elena knew where her husband was.

Sixto broadly smiled. "No. She was tired. She went right to sleep." He shrugged. "In the morning maybe I can get back to the bed before she wakes up."

"You don't have to set with me," Jawn Henry said.

Sixto nodded about that. "Suppose he comes back?"

"He ain't that dumb."

Sixto wagged a finger. "That might be what he wants folks to think. *Comprende*? People will not believe he will come back — but that would be the best time for him to do it. No?" Sixto stood up. "Is there coffee in the office?"

"On the shelf behind the stove . . . Sixto?"

"Qué?"

"You shouldn't even be out of bed."

The large man grinned. "You too. Well; do two cripples equal one bushwhacker? Let's wait and see."

Jawn Henry listened to the large man go up to the office. He was tired. By the time he got back with two cups of black joe Jawn Henry was sleeping like the dead so Sixto had to empty both cups.

Later, it got cold. Sixto went to sit on the other bunk in the cell and pull the old army blanket around his shoulders. Some hours later when Sixto opened his eyes Jawn Henry was watching him with an expression of amusement.

Sixto yanked straight up. "I just closed my eyes. For one moment. I hear like a coyote, even with my eyes closed . . . I'll make more coffee."

Jawn Henry watched the large man trail the old blanket like a Pima squaw as he left the cell. It did not hurt to laugh, providing he did not strain while doing it, so Jawn Henry laughed quietly.

Elena came to beat on the door. Her husband opened it and she exploded in his face. Jawn Henry heard but could not understand what she was saying, but anger is recognizable in any language. Jawn Henry eased down under his blankets and closed his eyes. He might just as well have remained sitting up. When Elena entered the cell with her husband in tow, she addressed the lump under the covers on the cot.

"Why didn't you send him home? Do you know he is not a well man? Constable, I didn't think you would do such a thing."

"Do what?" Jawn Henry said from beneath the blankets.

"Ah, you are awake. Do what? Take advantage of my sick husband instead of making him go home."

"He's bigger'n me, Elena. Besides I can't get out of bed."

"You got out of bed. The *curandera* told me." She paused. "Two sick men with no sense between them. Sixto, we will go home. Come along."

Jawn Henry risked peeking from beneath the blankets. Sixto turned, saw him, made a very elaborate shrug and followed his wife.

Jawn Henry heard them close the roadway door. He examined the six-gun Sixto had left, found it fully loaded, and sat with it in his lap until Raine Cotswol walked in, met no-one in the office and came down into the cell-room where he was met by an aimed and cocked six-gun in the constable's hand. The older man sighed, raised his eyebrows and waited until Jawn Henry allowed the Colt to lie in his lap.

Raine knew townsmen had brought back his dead riders. He had also heard of the attempt on Jawn Henry's life. He had even been told his rider named Maxwell had left Stillwater heading south. "On one of my horses, the son of a bitch," Raine Cotswol exclaimed. Then asked a question. "Did you know

136

the feller who tried to kill you last night?"

"Sort of. Jericho."

"What about Carl Maxwell?"

"He stole a horse in Mex-town exactly as I told you at the ranch. He rides with Jericho's renegades. I can't say why he got himself hired on by you; what I *can* tell you is that Maxwell out at the cow-camp is the same Maxwell the outlaw."

"I'll hang him," Raine exclaimed.

"Suits me," agreed the constable, "but you got to wait until I can stand up before you try it."

"You told me one time you didn't hold with lynchin'."

"I don't. If you find Maxwell . . . I told you this one time . . . I don't want to know what you did to the son of a bitch. Not one damned word."

"Then what difference does it make whether you can stand up or not?"

"Because I'm honour-bound to stop lynchings without no hearing an' no trial."

Old Cotswol's expression changed completely. "Then you'll never know. Now I got to see what I can turn up and hire a couple more riders."

Jawn Henry was not deluded. At the moment he was no match for old Raine Cotswol and had to leave it that way.

If it was humanly possible to find Carl Maxwell, old Raine would do it, regardless of the direction Maxwell had taken. Jawn Henry had meant what he had said. He never wanted to hear Maxwell's name again. But he would.

The *curandera* arrived about noon. She had a bottle of blood-red wine in her satchel which she opened and half-filled a glass for the constable and did the same for herself.

It was the best wine Jawn Henry had ever tasted, but granted he was far from being an authority on wine. He told the *curandera* it was a fine wine. Her response was given in the cryptic tone she had come to use toward Jawn Henry.

"It is from my cousin's vineyard down in Chihuahua. He is very proud of his wines. I'll see that he hears what you said. He will be pleased."

As the woman talked she was unwrapping bandages.

She stood gazing at the wound for a long moment before rummaging in her satchel of gatherings and speaking at the same time. "I never question the hand that dispenses miracles."

She turned and leaned down, holding a scrap of cloth soaked in some medicine. "There is still no sign of blood-poisoning . . . which there should be."

"When was the last time you had an all-over bath?"

Jawn Henry thought back. Knowing about her remark the previous night and seeking to avoid another outburst, he answered, "Week, maybe a tad more."

The hefty woman, her head lowered as she doctored the wound, quietly said, "Then it has to be a miracle," and straightened up. "The place you tore open . . . I can hardly tell it from the place that didn't tear open."

They emptied the bottle, and the *curandera* became mellow enough to say, "With a bath, a shave and a shearing you wouldn't be a bad-looking man, constable."

He smiled at her. "There's a mail-order house back east that sells glasses," he told her.

It sailed straight over her head. "Some day," she told him, stoppering the empty wine-bottle and gathering her other things, "you will have a woman. Let me tell you *compadre*, beware ones that are too thin, or that don't have lines in their faces from laughing, or that can't cook. Other things are important too, but . . . " The *curandera* shrugged, turned and went out into the little corridor where she said the rest of it before hiking up to the roadway door.

"She must make the floor shake when she walks, and she must bring with her warm bulk for cold winter nights."

Jawn Henry listened to the roadway door close, closed his eyes and slept — with the gun Sixto brought in his right hand atop the blankets.

8

Cotswol's Backfire

THE day was hot when Jawn Henry was finally able to go to the tonsorial parlour, get the key to the bath-house out back along with a threadbare towel and a chunk of tan lye soap.

He had a splendid scar and had lost considerable weight. Otherwise he felt fine, even though the injured leg occasionally let him know it was down there.

The town'd had time to pretty well forget its earlier excitement; other events had transpired to catch folks' interest. One of them was Raine Cotswol being raided in the night. He had lost about twenty beeves. The tracks led arrow-straight toward the Mexican border. They did not

142

deviate. Raine rode with Constable Mulligan and four riders he had hired to replace the men buried out behind Stillwater, and he was ready to froth at the mouth. Not that he couldn't stand the loss but being a cowman he just naturally breathed fire and brimstone when rustlers raided him.

For the constable it was the first long horseback ride he'd made since being injured. Lying in a bed robbed a man of some of his worthwhile needs, one of which was to go horsebacking, especially when it had to do with cattle thieves.

He was not hopeful but kept that to himself. The border was not far south, the raiders had at least a twelve-hour head start, and even assuming — correctly — that cattle could not be driven as hard nor as rapidly as stolen horses, that much lead almost certainly guaranteed the rustlers would get over the line down into Mexico before Raine's riders got close enough to see dust.

He had never ridden with Cotswol before and that made it possible for him to theorize about Raine leading his riders into that bushwhack up north.

On a trail, mad as a hornet, Raine did not use precaution. Back yonder it had caused several deaths. Riding over flat, desert country toward the Mex border now, while there were many places for an ambush to be set up, Cotswol rode as though obsessed with just one thing — finding the thieves. He ignored caution completely. His new hired men occasionally exchanged glances and rolled their eyes, but no ambush occurred, which Jawn Henry attributed more to the haste of the rustlers to get over the line down into Mexico than to any desire to waste time bushwhacking the pursuit.

They did not turn back until two days later when the clear sign of Cotswol critters being driven across the border stopped Raine in his tracks, glaring down into Mexico.

For Jawn Henry the entire ride had

been a way to test just how thorough his recovery had been. The fourth night when he rode into town, most folks were abed, but the saloon had lights showing.

The following morning Jawn Henry discovered how subtle pain could be. It had not bothered him the full period of time he had ridden with Raine, but the morning of the fifth day, when he rolled out of bed, every muscle in his body ached.

Oddly enough, his mended leg hurt least of all, even though the scar showed a heightened shade of red.

He had an early breakfast, crossed to the jailhouse for another cup of primer, then had barely got seated at his desk when Sixto Erro walked in, beat off clouds of dust with his hat and sank into a chair. "My cousin from Chihuahua came by yesterday with his pack-train." Sixto, who never hurried even when speaking, gazed at the toes of his boots briefly before raising his head to tell the rest of it.

"He found a dead man west of here a few miles . . . hanging in the only tree in sight."

Jawn Henry had a premonition. "Did your cousin cut him down?"

"No. But someone did, and buried him beneath the tree. I rode over there yesterday. My cousin said he was a *vaquero*, but even his spurs had been taken."

"You found the grave?"

"*Si*, but it wasn't much; mounded rocks piled atop him. This time of year digging in the ground — certainly digging deep enough for a grave — can't be done easily even if men have good tools."

"Then no-one knows who hanged him or even what his name was, eh?"

"His name was Maxwell."

Jawn Henry's brows shot up. "Maxwell was rustlin' cattle?"

"I don't know, but if you wish I can lead you to the grave." Sixto shot up to his feet, and smiled. "All I can tell you is that someone hung him."

"Before or after Cotswol lost his cattle?"

"I don't know much about that. Only what I heard in Mex-town," Sixto said, then narrowed his eyes in thought before also saying, "When did he lose the cattle?"

"Four, five days ago."

"No, *amigo*, this one was hanged and buried before that. How long before I don't know, but when my cousin found him in the tree he told me *sopilotes* had already been picking at the body."

After Sixto departed Jawn Henry went over to the saloon, nodded around, but had only one jolt by himself before going up to the rooming-house where he sat on the veranda for a long time.

There were pieces to the Maxwell puzzle he could not fit together. The foremost piece was how long Carl Maxwell had been dead. The second piece was why in Gawd's name wasn't Maxwell farther away since he'd obviously fled about the time Jericho had tried to kill Jawn Henry?

There were other pieces. He gave up, bedded down early and visited the tonsorial parlour right after breakfast the following day, had a shave and a shearing, went over to the jailhouse where he fired up the little office stove to brew coffee.

Raine Cotswol walked in about noon, dusty, sweaty and out of sorts. He dropped his hat beside the chair, dug out a huge blue bandana to mop his face with, then said, "It's gettin' to be a habit. They got fifteen head more cattle last night, but by Gawd from now on they'll get a surprise. I hired three men to hide out an' bed down with the cattle, an' had the best critters drove close to where they'll be waitin'." Cotswol wrinkled his nose. "Is that coffee hot?"

Jawn Henry gestured. "Help yourself. There's cups on the shelf," and as the cowman was filling a cup the constable asked a question. "They found Carl

Maxwell, but maybe you'd know about that, eh?"

Cotswol turned with pot in one hand, half-full cup in the other hand. If he'd been an actor he couldn't have registered more surprise. He held the cup down, went to the chair, sat and said, "Where?"

"West a-ways. He'd been hung, an' afterwards cut down and buried beneath a mound of boulders."

Cotswol tasted the coffee, which was too hot so he put the cup on the corner of Jawn Henry's desk. "How far west? Hell, he's had weeks to get plumb out of the territory."

Jawn Henry agreed. "For a fact. I think he died maybe ten miles west of here."

Raine's face wrinkled until every crease deepened. He stared at Jawn Henry. "A man could crawl that far, Jawn Henry."

"Yes, he could. Unless he had a good reason not to be no further."

Cotswol tried the coffee again, it was

still too hot. "That son of a bitch," Cotswol exclaimed with feeling. "He worked for me. He knew every band of my critters, where they grazed an' bedded. I got half a notion to dig him up an' hang him again."

Jawn Henry let that pass; it was the talk of a very angry man. "Raine, if he was ridin' with your rustlers — "

"If gawdammit, if. Why else would he still be in the country? It'll be him an' that subbitch who tried to shoot you. That 'breed, whatever his name was."

"Jericho?"

The older man glared; this time he half drained the coffee-cup before speaking. "I'm goin' to trap them if it's the last thing I ever do."

Cotswol stamped out of the office, went up to the saloon to join his latest hired hands in one jolt before getting astride and leaving town with his riders in a cloud of dust.

Jawn Henry kicked back at the desk, gazing at the ceiling. If Jericho had been with Maxwell — what had happened that one got hanged and the other one didn't? And — how many rustlers were being led to Cotswol country to make those raids? Were they Mex border-jumpers or maybe gringo renegades?

For the ensuing two days Jawn Henry rode over the country where the rustlers had been, found plenty of tracks, decided there were five or six men doing the raiding, stumbled onto the rock mound below the only tree for miles, sat gazing at it briefly before heading for town.

All he'd discovered was the number of men in the rustler band, the grave, and nothing else. It was one of those tantalizing riddles that would not let a man sleep.

Jawn Henry's leg no longer bothered him as it would fifteen years hence, but that was something he would have to experience later. At the present time he sprouted an eye in the back of his head, and aside from his customary shell-belt and holstered Colt, he carried

151

that big-bored little derringer.

If indeed Jericho had been working with Maxwell, stealing cattle would only be Jericho's pastime. He would only still be in the country because he had to kill a man.

Jawn Henry was out back cuffing his saddle-animals when Father Ruiz came back there. It was hot; they went inside where three-foot thick adobe walls kept the jailhouse cool. The priest said, "You know Carlos Aguirre — the man who had that horse stolen from him some time back?"

Jawn Henry nodded. He knew Aguirre, not as well as others in Mex-town. "What about him?"

"He trapped that same horse again."

"The horse Cotswol's rider took in broad daylight?"

"Yes. And now he worries. That the *vaquero* will steal him back again."

"No," Jawn Henry said dryly. "He's dead."

It was the priest's turn to be surprised. "Dead?"

"An' buried, father. That's all I know except that if Carlos loses that horse again it won't be Maxwell who steals it."

Later, along toward supper-time, Jawn Henry had little difficulty guessing about the horse. It had either gotten loose or had never been hobbled when its owner had been lynched. Every horse had a homing instinct; with most of them it was slight but with others it was strong. Evidently Maxwell's animal had returned to the place where it had been fed and watered, but however he had managed this did not really matter much. Except for one thing — his being loose pretty well clinched the fact that the man under the rock mound was Maxwell.

★ ★ ★

Raine Cotswol's cold, calculating anger worked, not entirely in the way the old cowman expected, but well enough. When the raiders appeared on barefoot horses so there would be no noise moving over rocky ground, they did not scout up the countryside, either because they expected to cut out cattle fast and drive them south the same way, or because they were careless. But in either case they came across open country with a scimitar moon at their backs, topped out over a low land-swell studying the bunched gather of fat animals, and this was their greatest error; those hand-selected cattle should have set off alarms in the back of their heads; but again, these were fine, beef animals. The six raiders eased down off the swell — below which were three heavily-armed men who had been awakened with the arrival of the thieves, and who had crept up the slope after the raiders moved down toward the cattle.

It wasn't a fair fight, it was murder. The raiders were fanning out to begin the drive when the shooting started. Two raiders were killed in their saddles, two more screamed, hooked their horses

154

hard and rode low. Each one of them was hit before they got out of sight in darkness.

Two raiders, already east of the cattle to keep them moving in the right direction, were too distant to provide good targets. They did as the pair of wounded men had done, hooked their horses hard and raced southward bent over their saddles.

The cattle stampeded in all directions. The firing was heard at the camp where Raine roused his other men, who bridled their horses, slammed on saddles, cinched up and rode toward the low side of the landswell where his other riders had ambushed the rustlers.

Raine listened to what the gunmen had to say, then without a word led his entire crew on the track of the raiders, which was southerly, the direction the rustlers had taken on previous raids.

They did not catch the men who had escaped unhurt, but they did come upon a head-hung horse whose reins were in the hand of a gunshot victim, a Mexican whose pearl-handled six-gun was appropriated by a Cotswol rider. They propped the wounded man up, opened his jacket and shirt so Raine could examine the wound by the light of a sulphur match then gave him water from a canteen. He drank, handed back the canteen and spoke to Cotswol in Spanish. "I will die, no?"

Raine had no pity. "*Si*, you will die. Where did you take my cattle?"

"To *Mejico*."

"Why? Who was your *jefe*?"

"To sell them to gringo cowmen down there who want better cattle than our kind. Big *rancheros*. We deliver the cattle, they pay us, and nothing more is said . . . do you have *pulque*?"

"No, we got no liquor. Who was your *jefe*?"

"He is called Juanico. He comes from your country."

Dawn was coming. The dying *vaquero* squinted as he said, "There is no moon, *señores*. It is very dark."

Raine Cotswol reached, pushed slightly; the Mexican toppled sideways with both eyes wide open, staring.

They left that one where he had died. Raine led the relentless pursuit. As the sky steadily brightened and the air was still chilly, they came upon another Mexican. His horse was nowhere in sight. He had a torn, bloody sleeve on the right side which he had tied off with a rawhide hatband.

When the riders appeared, gaining fast, the Mexican dropped behind a thick bush. Raine held up his hand. They walked their horses and stopped where Raine figured was about the range of a six-gun. He called ahead in Spanish. "Arise, rider of other people's horses. Leave the gun on the ground."

The Mexican neither stood up nor released his grip on his Colt.

Raine called once more. "Listen to me, son of a road-runner. We don't have to fight you, just sit down until your tongue gets fat from thirst. Come out in my sight — *now!*"

Still the Mexican did not appear.

Raine gestured for his riders to go out and around the thicket. "Keep out of gun range. When you can see him don't shoot the son of a bitch. I want him alive."

As the rangemen drifted away to encircle the area where the raider was hiding, Raine rode closer and called for the last time.

"Leave the gun, come out with your hands high . . . we will kill you if you don't come out."

The wounded man saw riders encircling him. He also understood that the craggy old gringo who had called to him meant exactly what he had said. He called back in Spanish, "You will kill me anyway, so it is better to die fighting."

Raine's answer to that was curt. "We're not goin' to kill you unless you make us do it. I want you alive. For the last time — *come out of them bushes!*"

The raider had no reason to believe

he would not be killed, except that the craggy old man who had called to him had said he would not be killed. It was little more than a straw, but the raider had nothing else, so he slowly arose with both hands above his head. He was a dark, short, stocky man with a badly pockmarked face. His age was indeterminate but a fair guess would have put him in his forties. There was an excellent chance he did not, himself, know how old he was.

Raine rode up, clasped both hands on the saddle-horn and studied the raider from cold eyes. He asked if the man spoke English. The Mexican nodded. "*Si*, yes." It was not entirely true; the man spoke border-English which was liberally sprinkled with Spanish, and even some Mexican-Indian words. But he could be understood.

He said his name was Maria Ramirez, that he was a deserter from the Mexican army. In an unusually forthright admission he also said he and the others had raided Cotswol cattle six times, which made eyes widen among the Cotswol men. All they knew about was three raids, counting the one that had ended in the capture of Maria Ramirez.

Raine did not dismount as he questioned the raider. "Where did your friends go?" he asked.

Ramirez gestured with his uninjured arm. "To the border and beyond."

"Who is your leader?"

"Juanico. He is not a Mexican. It is said he is a North American."

"Where, in Mexico, will he go now?"

Maria Ramirez shrugged. "That I cannot tell you. Before we were attacked Juanico said he would meet at the village of Saint Dolores which is about ten miles south of the border. But maybe he won't go there now."

"Why?"

"Why? Because you might go across the border to chase him."

Raine finally dismounted. His men did the same. Raine told someone to look after Ramirez's arm, turned his

160

back and told the other riders he would take the prisoner to Stillwater, hand him over to the constable. He wanted the others to stay on the trail of the raiders, but if they had to cross down into Mexico to be very careful. Peasants down there ambushed gringos for their horses, their guns, even their boots.

He had Ramirez's arms tied behind his back, had him boosted behind the saddle, nodded and grunted then started at a dead walk for Stillwater. His hired hands took up the southerly trail which was easy to read with the sun up and climbing.

For the full distance to Stillwater Raine did not say a word to the sweating man riding double with him, and Ramirez, who had read Cotswol correctly, made no attempt to break the silence.

9

Information

JAWN HENRY had only recently returned from an early supper when Cotswol arrived with his bloody captive. Raine pushed Ramirez into the jailhouse before releasing his arms. Ramirez, who had been in pain since being winged, sank upon a bench nursing the arm, which was swelling.

Jawn Henry watched the Mexican while Raine told him of the circumstances surrounding his capture and injury. Jawn Henry got his medicine-box, told the prisoner to remove his shirt, and without a word went to work cleaning the wound, making sure the lead had gone completely through flesh without touching bone, made a serviceable bandage, cut the arm out of the

Mexican's shirt and told him to put the shirt on.

Throughout all this Raine Cotswol had sat in stony silence. When Jawn Henry returned to his desk and wiped both hands on a large blue bandana, Cotswol said, "The leader of 'em is someone named Juanico.

Jawn Henry regarded the cowman stolidly. "Jericho."

Cotswol's eyes widened. Up until now he hadn't made the connection. In Spanish the letter j is pronounced something like 'ho' or 'wha'. Cotswol turned slowly to face Ramirez, but he was speaking to the constable when he said, "I'll be switched. All right, beaner, describe Juanico."

Ramirez replied forthrightly. "He is maybe a little taller than me. He is dark too, but not as dark as I am. He seems to be young, but I don't know about that. He speaks English like one of you . . . he hates gringos."

It wasn't an altogether reliable description, but it was good enough for the lawman and the rancher.

Jawn Henry leaned forward on the desk. "Where is he?"

Ramirez shrugged. He honestly did not know where Juanico might be after he had led his men into an ambush.

Ramirez replied using Spanish that sounded like 'yo no say'. Cotswol growled at him. "English, you son of a bitch. Use English."

Ramirez obeyed. "I don't know. He is *coyote*. He might be anywhere." Ramirez looked at the cowman. "Your riders won't find him. Nobody finds him if he don't want them to." Ramirez asked for whiskey. His arm was very painful. Jawn Henry dug a bottle from a low drawer, wordlessly handed the bottle to the wounded man, watched him swallow three times, took back the bottle and stowed it. Ramirez seemed to brighten, for a fact his sweating increased.

Jawn Henry asked how they could catch Juanico and Ramirez looked the constable straight in the eye and shrugged. "You can't. You will never catch him. He is smarter than a coyote. No gringo will catch him."

Jawn Henry returned the Mexican's steady gaze when he replied, "We'll catch him. Maybe we got to go to the ends of the earth but we'll catch him."

Ramirez gingerly moved his arm. Pain hit him like a hard blow. He clenched his teeth and fought not to show in his face how bad the pain was.

Someone lifted the *tranca* from the roadway side and walked in. It was the hefty *curandera*. She looked at all three of them before she put her satchel on the desk, turned her back to the lawman and the cowman, went over to the seated prisoner and examined his arm. When she was satisfied no bones had been broken she turned on Jawn Henry. "Why didn't you call me?"

Cotswol resented the woman's attitude and replied sharply, "Because we didn't need you. The constable done a right good job without you."

Jawn Henry saw the explosion coming, saw Raine Cotswol brace for it, and spoke coldly to the woman. "Do what you got to do. I only bandaged the bastard because you wasn't around."

The woman snorted, put her back to the lawman and Raine Cotswol and went to work removing the bandaging.

Raine looked at Jawn Henry and rolled his eyes. Jawn Henry eased back in the chair. Raine told Jawn Henry he had sent his riders on the trail of the rustlers. He did not say whether he had told them to cross the border if they had to, but Jawn Henry looked bleakly at the older man and asked about that.

Raine resettled in the chair, looked down to be reassured his hat was still on the floor, and finally put his full attention upon the *curandera* and her patient.

Jawn Henry said, "You did, didn't you? If they go south of the border there's a good chance they'll get picked up by the *rurales*."

Rurales were Mexico's constabulary corps. Mounted units which were a law unto themselves. They were efficient, experienced, and quite often deadly since they had the authority to apprehend bandits, or use the back roads into towns, apprehend and execute anyone making *tiswin*, *pulque* or *cerbeza*.

Cotswol gazed at Maria Ramirez as though he had not heard the constable. Jawn Henry blew out a rough sigh. "Raine if they get picked up down there, an make a fight of it, they could damned well start another war between us and Messico."

Still the older man seemed not to have heard, but the *curandera* had. She straightened up with both hands on her hips, glaring at the cowman. Cotswol picked up his hat, ducked out the roadway door, mounted his horse and cut across empty weed-patches to leave town on a southwesterly course.

The *curandera* turned on Jawn

Henry. "What idiot said people get smarter when they get old?"

Jawn Henry leaned back eyeing the hefty dark woman. "How about infection?" he asked mildly. The *curandera* turned back toward the Mexican, mumbled something to him in Spanish, listened, faced the desk and said, "His name is Maria Ramircz."

"I know his name," exclaimed Jawn Henry.

The woman also said, "He was with someone named Juanico when they hanged a gringo."

Jawn Henry came forward on the chair. "Ask him if the man they lynched was named Maxwell."

Before the woman could turn and interpret, Ramirez vigorously nodded his head.

"Ask why Maxwell got hung."

This time the forthright captive ignored the translator. "It was something about Maxwell running out on Juanico when he was supposed to help him kill someone in this town."

That did not surprise Jawn Henry. He still needed an answer about something else. "Why was Maxwell still in the country after he fled from this town?"

Ramirez spread his hands, palms up. He did not know anything beyond what he had just said. Jawn Henry believed him. If he was ever to get an answer to this, it would have to come from Jericho himself.

The *curandera* finished, wiped her hands, closed her satchel and faced the desk. "What will you do with this one?" she asked.

Jawn Henry did not reply. He arose with the ring of keys in his hand, jerked his head for Ramirez to precede him and went down into the cell-room. After locking the prisoner in and returning to his office, he shrugged because the *curandera* was gone. He would not miss her.

The day was wearing along. It was too late to go scouting for Raine or his riders. The latter would already be too far south, and while he might overtake Cotswol, since he now had most of the answers he had wanted he had no reason to find the old stockman.

He went over to Mex-town, to the *cantina* on the west side of the plaza where idlers, old men and a scattering of Mexicans from below the border gathered to sip wine, drink beer, smoke and talk.

His arrival did not entirely cause all conversation to die, but there was less talk than there had been. Jawn Henry got a glass of tepid red wine, found a chair and sat down, leaned back, eyed the other customers, most of whom he at least knew by sight, and sipped wine.

The proprietor, a short, heavy man given to profuse sweating from any exertion, came over to ask if Jawn Henry was looking for someone, or just visiting.

Jawn Henry smiled, said it was the latter, and his answer seemed to ameliorate the wariness; men went back to talking freely, except for one man whose saddle-warped legs were troublesome at the knees. He used a shiny old red manzanita stick when he walked. He used it to reach Jawn Henry's table, leaned and spoke in soft Spanish. "Companion, the man you are looking for has a woman in the house west of Sixto Erro's corral." The old man straightened up, leaned on his stick and also said, "Don't leave. Not for a long time after I've gone. You understand?"

Jawn Henry understood, barely nodded, continued to sip his wine without so much as watching the old informer's progress to the doorway, sat loose for almost a half-hour before he finally took his glass to the counter, placed it over there, trickled silver for the wine and departed.

Immediately voices buzzed. The barman looked down his nose when someone approached him at the bar. It was Mex-town's saloonman's dilemma, which he shared with all saloonmen, that his profession required him to listen to speculations with which he rarely agreed.

The man who leaned on the bar and spoke in a lowered voice was pulpy, elderly, with a sly fox-face. He said, "I think the constable has an interest in that widow who lives next to Sixto."

The saloonman went along his bar to care for other patrons. His informer took the obvious rebuff in stride, left the saloon and shagged a diagonal course across the plaza to his little *jacal*.

He missed seeing the constable, who was entering Sixto's residence, which was just as well, otherwise he might have altered his gossip to include Jawn Henry and Sixto's wife.

Elena Erro was in good spirits. Her man was out in the corral milking a goat. She smiled about that. Even when trained to stand on a box while being milked made little difference when the milker was as large and heavy as Sixto Erro.

She sat Jawn Henry at a kitchen table, got him coffee and told him that while it was her duty to milk the goat, she had refused since Sixto had gotten out of bed when he wasn't supposed to, so now he could milk the goat for a week.

Jawn Henry listened politely, nodded about her small victory and led the conversation around to the widow-woman who lived nearby.

Elena, who was not by nature a gossip, was nevertheless a woman. She told Jawn Henry the woman's name was Dulce Esparta, that her husband had died six years earlier, that she had no children — but had many friends. The word 'friends' was pronounced slowly while Elena Erro looked unblinkingly at the constable.

He emptied the cup, declined a refill and cleared his throat before describing Jericho and asking if Elena or Sixto had ever seen such an individual visit the widow.

Elena shrugged. "They mostly come

after dark. In poor light all but the very tall and the very short look alike. I don't know. If you wish we will watch."

Jawn Henry went out to the corral where Sixto straightened up with a grimace. Milking goats, even atop a box, was hard on the back. Jawn Henry could be less discreet with Sixto, who listened to everything the lawman had to say, then concentrated briefly on stripping the goat before getting her off the box and turning with the pail in his hand as he said, "It can't be the same man, Jawn Henry. Jericho would not be that foolish."

The constable did not argue but he did not agree. Many men had come to disaster because of their lack of good judgement where women were concerned. Jawn Henry asked if Sixto would watch the widow's place. Sixto agreed. They parted where Sixto took the path to the house and the constable veered off for his return to Gringo-town.

He had a late supper, bedded down early and arose the following morning the same way. He fed Ramirez, left the jailhouse key with the paunchy individual who operated the emporium, saddled up and rode south-west with blessed coolness all around.

The ride to Cotswol's cow-camp was as long as a rider elected to make it. Jawn Henry did not lift his animal out of a walk for several miles, then he only loped a short distance. He was not sure Raine would be at the camp.

He wasn't, but an ailing rider was. The man had got so thirsty a few days back he had tanked up at a still-water pond with the predictable result that he now had an affliction known among stockmen and their riders as 'the green-apple quickstep'.

The rider could not say when Raine would return. He could not even say, with any degree of certainty, that any of them would ever return — not if they crossed down into Mexico.

It wasn't exactly a wasted trip but

neither was it productive. On the ride back Jawn Henry passed through midday heat, which was increasing by the moment. By the time he got back to Stillwater it was hot.

His animal was grateful for the shade and trough of his corral. Jawn Henry returned to the jailhouse, brought Maria Ramirez to the office, sat him down, got him coffee, then asked questions.

It was, actually, a pleasant hour for them both. Ramirez had a sense of humour. His arm was badly swollen but he shrugged off Jawn Henry's sympathy with words that epitomized an outlaw's philosophy.

"Every time a man rides out there is the face looking at you, smiling or crying."

Ramirez was comfortable, he had been fed and it was cool in the office. As time passed he related other raids, other escapades, other fights; but when Jawn Henry asked about the widow-woman over in Mex-town, Ramirez faintly scowled. He had never heard of Juanico having a woman, but then for as long as he had been riding with Juanico there had been few periods when they could rest.

Jawn Henry asked if Juanico having a woman might have something to do about why he was lingering in a country where folks wanted his scalp.

Ramirez admitted such a possibility existed but he, personally, knew nothing about Juanico and a woman — any woman.

Jawn Henry had returned him to his cell when the *curandera* arrived. He took her down to the cell, locked her inside with Ramirez after telling her that when she finished, if she made enough noise to be heard in the office he would release her.

Ramirez, on the edge of the bunk, was lecherously grinning. The hefty woman turned. She glared and told him if he tried it she would break both his arms.

Ramirez did not try it. He only had one using arm anyway.

Father Ruiz arrived trailing a tiny banner of dust from the roadway. He knew about Maria Ramirez and wanted to see him.

Jawn Henry told the priest he would have to wait, the *curandera* was with his prisoner. Father Ruiz's eyebrows shot straight up. "A *curandera*? Didn't you know they have the talent of witchcraft?"

Jawn Henry eyed his visitor. He had never heard of such a thing, although since arriving in Stillwater he had come to tolerantly accept a lot he thought was superstition. This did not however include the *curanderas*. He knew for a fact and from experience that whatever their hocus-pocus, it worked.

The hefty woman called, Jawn Henry went down to let her out of Ramirez's cell, and when she stepped into the office the priest crossed himself. She glared, stormed to the roadway door, let herself out and slammed the door.

Jawn Henry took the priest down to Ramirez's cell, but did not allow the holy man to go inside as he had done with the medicine-woman.

Much later, with shadows thick and barely noticeable less heat, Jawn Henry went over to the cafe, and got a surprise; Raine Cotswol was already having supper. His appearance though suggested he had not been in town long. He was layered with dust, had drying sweat on his shirt and cracked lips.

He exchanged a nod with the constable and continued eating. Jawn Henry decided the stockman hadn't eaten for a considerable length of time, and paced his own meal so that they finished about the same time. Jawn Henry called for the cafeman to provide a pail of grub for one prisoner, then waited until he had the pail before joining Raine Cotswol, who was enjoying the diminishing heat while leaning on an upright post having a chew.

10

One Dead Man and an Uncertain Future

FATHER RUIZ was waiting. When Jawn Henry entered the jailhouse with Raine Cotswol the priest barely acknowledged the cowman as he addressed Jawn Henry.

"That man needs help."

Jawn Henry went to his desk, sat down and reared back. "The *curandera* was with him. She didn't say — "

"His arm is infected. He has a fever. It is blood-poisoning."

Raine Cotswol put a cold look on the priest. "You sure it's blood-poisoning?"

Father Ruiz turned on the older man. "Yes, I am sure. Do you think a priest only prays? They learn about illness and medicine too."

Cotswol reacted to the priest's sharp

tone as he always reacted to someone's anger. He said, "Let the son of a bitch die. You know who he is, what he's done — stole a lot of my cattle. We killed one, this one got shot through the arm an' we shagged the others to the border, where a company of *rurales* was camped over the line like they expected us."

Father Ruiz had only one concern. He appealed to Jawn Henry, "There is a medical doctor down at — "

Raine Cotswol came out of his chair cursing. "If he's really got blood-poisonin', let it kill him. As far as I know there's no doctor on earth who can save him — you damned black robe!"

Father Ruiz again addressed Jawn Henry. "He is a human being!"

Cotswol had an answer for that too. "He is a damned cattle-thievin' son of a bitch. Let me tell you somethin', mister, anyone tries to take Ramirez to a doctor won't never get there!"

Father Ruiz replied bitterly, "Constable,

you can't let him die. As a Christian your duty is to — "

Jawn Henry interrupted. "Ignacio, Mister Cotswol's right. Nothing will save his life if he's got blood-poisoning."

"Jawn Henry, you have to try. What kind of a Christian — "

Cotswol opened the door so hard it struck the wall. He started toward the priest. Father Ruiz stepped swiftly around him and left the jailhouse.

Raine closed the door, sat down and blew out a rough sigh. "I never could stand 'em, snivellin' bunch of whiners."

Jawn Henry eyed the older man. "They got a job to do just like the rest of us."

Cotswol flared again. "You a church-goer, Jawn Henry?"

"No, but they got a right to their beliefs. Now tell me about those rustlers."

"I already told you. They got down over the line an' my riders was stopped by *rurales* who seemed to be waitin' for

182

someone to chase them danged thieves down into Messico."

After the irate cowman left, Jawn Henry sat a long time with both hands clasped behind his head. He had never heard of Mexican regulars being tied in with rustlers, but he would not rule out that possibility. Whether it was a fact or not, Raine Cotswol would never see his stolen beef again, and that was a damned fact. Cattle and horses driven down into Mexico were not recovered, not even when protests were lodged through US authorities to Mexico City.

Jawn Henry returned to Mex-town in search of Father Ruiz. He found the priest watering tomato-plants in the old mission garden. For this work Ignacio Ruiz had the hem of his robe hoisted and his sleeves up to his elbows. He nodded to Jawn Henry and continued to pour water from a wooden bucket over the tomato-plants.

Jawn Henry leaned on the garden gate as he said, "Ignacio, he's lost a lot of cattle to those thieves. You got to understand how you'd feel in his boots."

The priest straightened up. "Jawn Henry, that man is an infidel. It will be on his head if Ramirez dies."

The constable replied quietly, "Ignacio, if Ramirez dies of blood-poisoning it will be his own fault. He stole cattle. He's been an outlaw for fifteen years. He told me about some of the raids he rode into."

"But he remains a human being."

"Sure he does, but what happened was his own fault. No-one forced him to become an outlaw. If he dies it will be his own fault. Tell me somethin', father, do you know a woman named Dulce Esparta?"

"Yes, I know her. She comes to services now and then.

"You know her reputation?"

The priest sighed. "Yes, I know. I pray for her. Now you are going to tell me what she does is wrong. You would be right — but she is one of our sheep. We can't judge her. That's for God to do."

Jawn Henry straightened up off the gate. "God an' Raine Cotswol," he said mildly. "I'm talkin' about Ramirez. God an' Raine Cotswol will pass judgement."

"It's not the same thing," exclaimed the holy man.

Jawn Henry thought otherwise. "Sure it is. Stealin' livestock or doin' what she does are both wrong. Goodnight, Ignacio."

The following morning Jawn Henry was heading for the cafe where the only light showed behind a steamed window, when a rifle sounded. Where the bullet struck, six inches from Jawn Henry, it would not be light enough to see the puncture in a wood wall for another hour or so.

Jawn Henry sprang into a recessed doorway, six-gun up and ready as its owner scanned the opposite side of the road.

There was wispy, shadowy movement

atop the harness-maker's building, but there was insufficient light. Jawn Henry was unable to catch more than shadowy motion before the movement stopped being visible.

He crossed the road in a run, ducked down through a weed-patch between two buildings, got out into the west-side alley as swiftly as possible — which was not swift enough. He heard the running horse up near the north end of the alley.

By the time he had gone north to the upper end of town he could no longer hear the horse.

He turned back as far as the rooming-house, heard aroused people farther south calling back and forth after having heard the gunshot, ignored that, went to his room and stood looking out through the window.

That damned 'breed was not down in Mexico or, if he had been, he hadn't remained there any longer than to get a fresh animal and return. Cotswol was right about one thing, Jawn Henry would have to sprout an eye in the back of his head.

Jawn Henry left Stillwater just at sunrise, picked up fresh tracks north of town, and when they veered around westerly he followed them until the sun was climbing then returned to town. The tracks had made a big sashay around the west side of town and had finally gone arrow-straight toward the border. There was no reason to shag tracks that far, Jawn Henry was satisfied about the identity of the bushwhacker.

The first visitor to the jailhouse after he returned was the *curandera*. She wanted to see the prisoner. Jawn Henry pointed to a chair. When she sat he told her about Father Ruiz's visit. She nodded; she had already heard about the priest's indignation. She looked steadily at the constable when she said, "He is right, your prisoner will die. The nearest doctor is sixty miles from Stillwater. That would be two days by stagecoach. Within two days he will be beyond help. He will die."

She arose, clutching her little satchel. "I will do all that can be done. Constable, when he gets bad, give him whiskey — all he wants — and say a prayer."

He took her down to Ramirez's cell, locked the door behind her, returned to his office, took a single pull from the whiskey bottle kept in a lower desk drawer and did not think about Maria Ramirez, but about Jericho — also known as Juanico.

There was not much he could do except sprout that eye in the back of his head — and hope the renegade would miss again if he tried to kill Jawn Henry after sundown.

But he was thoroughly satisfied the 'breed would not give up. He thought that Ramirez was correct. Jericho hated gringos.

When the topic came up over the following days about the mysterious gunshot, Jawn Henry passed it off. It was common for townsmen who had poultry to shoot raccoons, foxes, skunks, even upon occasion local dogs who raided hen-houses.

Sixto Erro came up from Mex-town with an interesting bit of information. That widow-woman named Esparta was visited the night the invisible gunman had tried to assassinate the constable.

Sixto did not know of the attempt, but Jawn Henry had little difficulty putting the two pieces together. He asked if Sixto knew Dulce Esparta. Sixto rolled his eyes. His wife, he said, would not even allow him to look over the corral fence in the direction of the Esparta *jacal*. But yes, he knew Dulce Esparta, but only because he had been a friend of her dead husband.

Jawn Henry leaned on the desk. "Who knows her well enough to ask when the man who visited her the other night will return?"

Sixto thought for several moments before answering. "Elena does, but she hasn't visited Dulce for many months. They grew up together. We — all four of us were close friends while her husband was alive . . . I don't know if Elena would do it. Her opinion of Dulce has changed a lot this past couple of years."

"I need to know when he will visit her again, Sixto."

"Why, *amigo*?"

"Because her visitor is Jericho an' I got a feelin' he visited her the night he tried to kill me."

Sixto digested that slowly. "An' now, if you know when he will return . . . ?"

"Yes."

Sixto arose. "I'll talk to my wife, but don't be surprised if she refuses."

Jawn Henry smiled a little. "Tell her why I have to know. Because Jericho snuck back up here the night he tried to kill me. Tell her if she will help, I may be around for your funeral."

Sixto grinned, winked and left the jailhouse.

Jawn Henry went down to see how his prisoner and the *curandera* were getting along, and was shocked at the sight of Maria Ramirez. His shirt

190

was soaked with sweat, his eyes were bright and seemed not to focus. He had changed incredibly over the last twenty-four hours.

The *curandera* passed out of the cell, waited until Jawn Henry had locked the door then made a snide comment. "You don't have to lock it. He's not going anywhere."

Up in the office she sat wearily on a bench with the satchel in her lap and regarded Jawn Henry solemnly. "I never seen it spread so fast," she said softly, almost as though she were talking to herself. "He will die by the day after tomorrow. Maybe even by tomorrow night." She arose. "I'll tell Father Ruiz."

After the *curandera* departed Jawn Henry sighed. Father Ruiz would be along directly wearing his shawl and carrying his little bundle of oil, tiny candles, and his good book.

Jawn Henry went down to see Ramirez. The outlaw was limp on the wall-cot, soaked with perspiration.

When Jawn Henry spoke, Ramirez's eyes flickered but he did not focus on the man upon the far side of his steel cage.

Jawn Henry tried twice more with identical results both times. Ramirez did not respond, but the last time he opened his eyes, stared through the constable, closed both eyes and continued his irregular breathing.

Jawn Henry returned to the office and true to his prediction Father Ruiz came in out of the dust and rising heat of another new day. He said, "The *curandera* told me."

Jawn Henry took the priest down to the cell, did not lock the door and told him to call out when he was finished. He returned to the office about the time the clerk from the general store brought his mail over, something which only happened when the storekeeper could no longer force things into the little pigeon-hole where Jawn Henry's mail was stored because it would not hold any more.

The post was usually uninteresting. This day was no different until he picked up the last letter. It was from a sheriff in Texas who had enclosed a Wanted dodger — this one with a picture on it — offering five hundred dollars reward for the arrest of one Jericho Quetzl. The dodger listed the crimes as six murders, three robberies, four charges of horse-and cattle-stealing and one charge of escape from a Texas prison.

Jawn Henry disposed of everything the clerk had brought but the Wanted dodger. He left that atop his desk to study when the priest called.

Father Ruiz said nothing until they were in the office with the door to the cell-room closed and barred, then he spoke in a subdued voice. "I thought twenty years ago I would get over it."

Jawn Henry waited.

"Death."

"Ramirez is dead?"

"No, but he is close to it. His mind is no longer rational, his eyes don't focus, his breathing is rapid, he is soaked with sweat. He did not hear a thing I said."

"What did you say?"

"I gave him last rites. There was no reason to prolong the visit. I will pray again at the mission. I think Mister Cotswol will be glad."

"Not glad, Ignacio — satisfied."

"Shall I notify the carpenter to have a box ready?"

"I'd appreciate it. And one other thing — let the *curandera* know, if you will."

The priest left with a noticeable drag to his usual brisk pace. Jawn Henry left the door open. The roadway was dancing with heat. In hot weather dead people should be buried as quickly as possible.

He went down into the cell-room to look through the steel straps at Maria Ramirez. The man was breathing but shallowly and irregularly. Jawn Henry said his name twice. He might as well have been speaking to the wall.

It was an unusual afternoon, beginning with the arrival of the *curandera*. Jawn Henry accompanied her to the cell where Maria Ramirez lay still. She bent over, blocking the constable's view as she said, "He is alive."

Jawn Henry edged around until he could see Ramirez. The man was soaked with sweat, his colour was high, his eyes were glazed and fixed. "Not for long," he said quietly.

The *curandera* threw him a venomous glare then rummaged in her satchel for medicine, in this case powders of some sort. She got the medicine down Ramirez only because there was water and someone to hold his head up so that he could swallow.

Jawn Henry eased the man down. "What did you give him?"

"Laudanum."

"That's not *curandera* medicine."

The glare again. "Any medicine is *curandera* medicine. This way he will ease out of life which may be better than you and I will do."

Ramirez stopped breathing. It was so quiet in the cell that the sound of birds fluttering around a mud nest built against the outside back wall was very audible.

The woman straightened up, made the sign of the cross on Ramirez's forehead, was briefly bowed, then turned on Jawn Henry. "He was not a bad man."

She seemed to be challenging the constable to a different answer. Jawn Henry surprised her. Looking at the peaceful countenance of the dead man he said, "None of us are at the end. Foolish, maybe; brought up hard, wanting to hate and cause suffering, but not bad."

"No? What then?"

"Unable to handle life," Jawn Henry replied and led the way back to the office.

The *curandera's* attitude had changed between the cell and the office. She actually smiled at Jawn Henry with the open door in her hand. "You would have made a good priest," she said, and left him gazing at the door after she departed.

Father Ruiz returned. Jawn Henry waited until he was seated before saying, "You told the *curandera*?"

The priest nodded looking defensive. "You disapprove?"

"No . . . Ramirez is dead."

The priest crossed himself. "The coffin will be ready in the morning. I'll take care of the burial."

Jawn Henry nodded and changed the subject. "Tell me something, Ignacio. Are the people in Mex-town likely to help Jericho?"

"If you mean will they hide him, no. Everyone down here knows about him, knows he is going to kill you." Father Ruiz paused. "Down there the people will likely always resent gringos, but they are, most of them anyway, in favour of justice — which, in your case, means they oppose the idea of bushwhacking."

Jawn Henry made a wry smile. Priests

seemed incapable of a simple yes or no. After the priest left, Jawn Henry went out back to look after his horse. He leaned on the topmost corral stringer for a long time before crossing to the cafe for a meal.

The cafeman was careful of his words when he said, "These are bad times, constable."

Jawn Henry nodded. All times are bad depending on who says they are. Sixto Erro walked in, sat next to the lawman, ordered and leaned to speak softly. "Did you find the grave?" he asked. Jawn Henry had found it. He also had it from Ramirez why Maxwell had been hanged, but all he said was, "Yeah, the tree and the mound of rocks. But anyone could be buried there."

Sixto looked offended. "I told you who it was."

Jawn Henry nodded. "I believed you. Anyway, Maxwell is out of it, dead or alive. Maybe I'll never know why the fool hung around when anyone in his fix with a lick of sense would have never looked back after he ran out on Jericho, but it don't really matter . . . where is Jericho?"

Erro spread large hands. "I don't know. I do know he's not in Mextown." Sixto leaned still closer to half whisper. "I have friends in Mex-town watching. If he comes they'll tell me. I'll tell you." Sixto moved to sit upright as his platter and coffee arrived. After the cafeman had walked away Sixto eyed his meal as he said, "He has to be a fool to think — even if he kills you — he will get away afterwards. Nobody likes bushwhackers.

Jawn Henry drained his cup and looked at the large, thick man. "I got a dead man in a cell across the road. I better get back in case the carpenter comes for him with his wheelbarrow."

Outside, another day was beginning to fade. The heat remained and would continue to do so until about midnight.

He went up to the saloon, which, because it was a weekday, had about a third the number of customers as it would have any Saturday.

Those two old men from the south end of town were sharing a bottle. Jawn Henry thought one or the other of them had got money somewhere and faced the barman to order a glass of beer; he had never been much of a drinker, something the barman had learned over the years.

The barman had few customers as he leaned his hips against the back-bar shelf, crossed his arms and said, "You like to buy a saloon, constable?"

Jawn Henry, expecting anything but this, widened his gaze at the barman. "You want to sell?"

The barman did not uncross his arms. "I expect, like every line of work, a man just eventually gets plumb tired of the same faces, the same rotgut, the same job day in an' day out. I'm not sure I want to sell but I sure-Lord need a month or such. It's a matter of bein' outdoors, not havin' to serve drinks, not having to listen to everyone's troubles."

Jawn Henry half-drained the beer glass. "Close up, take some time off. One thing I'd bet good money on is when you come back they'd be waitin'."

The saloonman abruptly changed the topic without uncrossing his arms or straightening up off the back-bar. "That 'breed, or whatever he is, is goin' to kill you if he can. Don't look so surprised. Hell, everyone up here'n down in Mextown knows that. Constable, maybe it's you needs time off; take a long ride for a few weeks. If the back-shootin' son of a bitch shows up in town again, if he was holdin' a stick he'd go to hell before the handle got cool."

Jawn Henry eventually bedded down and remained wide awake for a long time. If everyone knew Jericho figured to kill Jawn Henry, then by the very nature of future events casting shadows ahead, the attempt would be made soon — depending upon what Jericho believed would be his best opportunity.

Not on another rooftop this time; next time with better light and a stationary target.

He eventually slept, after considering his future course of action, which was simple enough — avoid places where a bushwhacker could make another attempt on his life.

And just how the hell did a man do that when the nature of his job required high visibility?

11

A Crisis

THEY buried Maria Ramirez in the paupers' section of Stillwater's cemetery with his name on the upright wooden slab. He would rest through eternity among others with similar markers, and about two dozen with markers without names.

Jawn Henry rode to the Cotswol cow-camp, arrived just shy of noon as the riders were returning for a meal, and learned from Raine Cotswol that a hard-riding band of Mexicans from below the border had made a pass at his camp, shot it up without hitting anyone because of darkness, and had continued on northward.

The generalization, based on fire-flashes from gun muzzles, was that there had been at least fifteen border-jumpers.

Raine and his riders had gone out among the cattle but this time, because the *bandolero*s' tracks did not deviate from a northward course, it was clear whoever the riders had been, they'd had some other purpose in mind than stealing Cotswol cattle.

On the ride back to Stillwater Jawn Henry cursed the telegraph people who had declined Stillwater's importunings that a telegraph office be established in town, because now he had no quick way to warn communities northward of a band of border jumpers being loose in the territory.

He neglected to mention any of this when he got back to town. Obviously the raiders did not have attacking Stillwater in mind, otherwise they would have struck by now, but if he mentioned what he had learned at the cow-camp, the townsmen would have forted up scairt out of their wits. There had been raids by large bands of *bandoleros* on just about all the border communities north of the line at one time or another. Their savagery had made lasting and deep impressions; just the mention of border-jumpers being in the territory could start wild speculations and encourage chaos.

He had been in his office less than an hour when those two old gaffers from the tar-paper-shack community at the lower end of Stillwater walked in sober as a pair of judges. One of them, whose name was Sam Mortenson, took the chair. His companion crossed to the wall bench. Mortenson wasted no time. "We was settin' up late last night — sometimes it's hard to sleep when a body's got aches in most every joint — anyway, me'n Herb was settin' up last night pretty late. We heard a solitary horseman come in from the south . . . well, you know most folks travel in daylight, but it didn't have to mean that this — "

Jawn Henry interrupted. "Sam, get to the point, will you?"

Mortenson dragged a soiled cuff across his lips before continuing. "There was this rider by hisself. We went outside. The light was poor. The moon was gone or somethin' maybe behind a cloud. Y'know how that is, Mister Mulligan."

Jawn Henry leaned on his desk with clasped hands.

The old man spoke again. "I'm gettin' to the point. Keep your shirt on. This solitary rider was astride a big brown horse with a roached mane. Like I said, the light was poor, but for a fact Herb'n me made out a neck brand."

Jawn Henry nodded. "Army horse?"

"Yes sir it was, but the rider wasn't no soldier so we figured he stole the horse."

Jawn Henry nodded again; it was a reasonable assumption. "Could you make him out?" he asked.

"Not real good, Mister Mulligan, except that he was about average height, carried a booted Winchester an' a belt-gun, pretty dark-skinned, like maybe a Messican or a 'breed."

"He passed the livery-barn. In fact

he never stopped at all until he was athwart the roomin'-house. Up there he sat his horse lookin' for a long time. Herb said he was fixin' to dismount. I didn't notice that, but anyway, some dogs barked an' he rode on up out of town to the north. Now then, Mister Mulligan, you roomin' at the hotel, an' us knowin' about some renegade wantin' your scalp, we just got to wonderin' . . . "

Jawn Henry thanked the old men for stopping by, saw them on their way in the direction of the saloon, sat at his desk a while then went over to Mex-town and found Sixto Erro shoeing a horse in pitiless shade, sweating like a stud woodtick and glad for any respite.

Sixto left the horse tied, sluiced off, came out of the corral and invited the constable to share some *cerbeza*. Jawn Henry trailed the larger man into *ramada*-shade and sat down but declined the offer of beer, waited until Sixto had got his own beer and was sweating comfortably in shade, then asked if Sixto had heard of border-jumpers being in the area.

The large man sipped beer, sprawled in the chair and smiled. "This morning I heard. I was comin' over to tell you when I finished shoeing the horse."

"Raine Cotswol was fired on last night when they passed. His guess is that there's maybe fifteen in the band."

Sixto emptied the bottle, heartily belched and settled more comfortably in the chair. "I don't know how many. All I know is that Carlos Aguirre an' another old man went out yesterday with burros to gather firewood. They had a dry camp in an arroyo. A band of Messicans rode by in a lope. The old men was scairt peeless. They said it was a lot of them an' they wore crossed bandoliers. They didn't have no scout an' they rode like men with a purpose an' a destination in mind." Sixto leaned to put the empty bottle aside. "*Bandoleros* are trouble, Jawn

Henry. Multiply it by fifteen an' that's a hell of a lot of trouble. But maybe not here if they kept ridin' north." Sixto discreetly belched wetly behind a huge hand, used his cuff and spoke as he was lowering the arm. "Why didn't they raid Stillwater? Everyone was asleep."

Jawn Henry had no answer to that. "From what I've gathered they rode like men with a destination in mind."

"Yes, but the farther they get from the border the greater their chances of never getting back down across it." Sixto shrugged. "It don't matter as long as it ain't us, does it?"

Jawn Henry could not quite agree with that, so he said, "An' Jericho rode through town last night."

That startled Sixto Erro. "You saw him?"

"No, them two old men from the lower end of town. The ones called Sam and Herb, saw him ride up through, hesitate near the rooming-house, then continue northward. Sixto, I got to wonderin' how much of a coincidence would it be for Jericho to ride through town the same night those border-jumpers shot up the Cotswol cow-camp an' kept on ridin'. Raine told me Jericho got down over the line before Raine's riders could catch him. He also told me there was a *rurale* detachment screening off the border after the surviving rustlers got down there."

Sixto squinted. "You think the *rurales* was down there to help the rustlers get clear, an' maybe to fight Cotswol's riders if they tried to chase the rustlers down into Messico?"

Jawn Henry hung fire before replying. "I ain't too worried about that. Maybe it was a coincidence, but — "

Sixto snorted.

Jawn Henry continued speaking. "An' maybe it wasn't no coincidence, but that's not what bothers me."

"What does?"

"Was Jericho part of the raider band? Did he cut loose from them to ride up through town with maybe some idea of shootin' me in bed?"

Sixto went to an olla, drank deeply and returned to his chair. "Jawn Henry," he said, speaking slowly, thoughtfully. "You don't want to keep on like you been doin', waitin' for him to sneak in and kill you. What you got to do is find the son of a bitch an' kill him first." Sixto wiped off sweat, reset his hat and leaned forward as he spoke softly. "You are sure he rode on up out of town last night?"

"That's what Sam an' Herb said. They saw him ride northward after barkin' dogs spooked him from near the hotel."

Sixto leaned back with a puckered brow before speaking again. "Well, maybe, but Elena woke me up last night. She said there was a horse stampin' over behind the Esparta house. I went to see. If she was right, by the time I got around there no horse was in sight."

Sixto put a dark look in the constable's direction, waiting for Jawn

Henry to speak. It was a long wait. "If it was Jericho," he finally said, "he could have rode with the raiders an' cut loose from them. The question is — did he visit *Señora* Esparta before or after the border-jumpers tried to shoot up Raine Cotswol's camp?"

Sixto found this matter of timing pointless. "He was here last night, so was the border-jumpers. You want to bet they come together?"

Jawn Henry arose wagging his head. "No. What I want to know is if he joined the border-jumpers somewhere up north — an', whatever they're up to, if they'll come back the same route they used goin' north. What I'd mostly like to know is — where is Jericho?"

Sixto also arose. "He'll be ridin' with them. I'll bet a good horse on that."

"You got a good horse, Sixto?"

"No. But I know where I can steal one."

They both laughed before Jawn Henry returned to Gringo-town with the sun slanting away.

Sixto Erro was solemn and silent through his late mid-day meal, and afterward told his wife nothing as he went down to the Mex-town cantina.

In hot weather it was always difficult to recruit riders, but the cantina was the best place to find men gathered who would listen to what Sixto had to say.

The result was predictably disappointing. There were only three young men at the cantina, the others were old and quite willing to have the world end tomorrow providing it happened after the heat arrived. They were unmoved, sympathetic but unmoved.

When Sixto returned to saddle his horse — which had shoes only on its front feet — his wife came out looking anxious. She asked where Sixto was going. He did not lie, he rarely lied to her, but his answer, which was obvious since he was saddling the horse, was not complete. She was accustomed to that too, so she stood under the *ramada* and watched him ride away.

He had said he was going riding. It was the truth, but not the whole truth.

As Sixto led his three young riders northwesterly he told them part of what they already knew — there were bandoleros in the area. What he also told them was that they were going to try and find them. This brought a sharp complaint from one *vaquero*. "We are only four men."

Sixto agreed. "I know that. We are going to find them — not fight them."

That calmed the younger man. It also had a sobering effect upon his companions. Tracking was not difficult — many border-jumpers left sign a blind man could read. Eventually, when they had covered some miles, Sixto sent two of his riders to scout ahead, one easterly and northward, the other westerly and northward. While they were in more or less open country, Sixto was wary of an ambush. He did not believe it would happen because from what he could read of the tracks, the border-jumpers appeared to have a destination in mind which precluded anxiety about being tracked. At least they did not slacken their pace nor spread out.

The nearest town was a place called Tres Pinos, about the size of Stillwater but with one advantage, the railroad passed through Tres Pinos. It was a thriving community with an economy roughly twice the size of Stillwater's economy. It possessed businesses Stillwater lacked such as a telegraph office, a train station and depot, a bank housed in a brick building and even three churches and an equal number of saloons.

By midday Sixto had begun to suspect Tres Pinos could be the destination of the border-jumpers because beyond Tres Pinos there were no additional settlements northward for over a hundred miles, and the *bandoleros* were riding arrow-straight in the direction of Tres Pinos.

Sixto was so engrossed in his tracking

he overlooked something — timing.

The border-jumpers had passed northward a good twenty-four hours before the men from Stillwater's Mex-town had taken up the trail.

He came face to face with this oversight when his scouts returned in a lope to report a large band of riders coming down-country from the direction of Tres Pinos. The scouts had seen them from a distance but they did not have to get closer, men riding distinctive Mexican saddles would only be Mexicans.

There was a moment of panic before Sixto led the withdrawal, going eastward in order to take full advantage of what skimpy cover there was.

One Mex-town rider remained back a short distance to watch for the border-jumpers. If he was seen it would probably cause no concern; this was cattle country, riders were likely to be abroad, even as many as three or four in a group which, in any case, posed no threat to fifteen hard-riding bandoleros whose vocation was killing.

Sixto did not see the bandoleros even after he got into what skimpy brush-cover the countryside provided. One of the younger men reined in beside Sixto to wonder aloud if the bandoleros might not attack Stillwater on their way back over the border to safety.

Sixto did not think they would but sent the young rider hurrying ahead to warn Jawn Henry and everyone else the border-jumpers were returning.

Again, he speculated about their purpose in riding north, and now in hurrying back the way they had come. The reason probably should have occurred to him but right at this moment he only worried about being seen, chased and attacked and in warning Stillwater the bandoleros were coming in the direction of the town.

They loped steadily but still were eventually able to see dust far back. The Mexicans were making good time, too good for riders who had passed northward with haste, unless they had got fresh horses somewhere.

Sixto's companions did not slacken their gait, not with that dust to encourage their retreat. None was a coward but neither were any of them fools. Fifteen to four was daunting odds.

The sun had swung westerly without being noticed to have done so. The heat was dry and leaching, the kind of heat that pulled sweat out of men and animals, even those standing still. Those moving at a lope sweated more.

Sixto did not like to do it but he called for his riders to pick up the gait. Far back he could make out ant-sized riders who had gained on Sixto because they were riding faster.

A companion swung in beside Sixto. He was less dark than the others, with black hair and eyes. He was sweat-shiny but smiling as he called to the older man, "What kind of horses do they breed in Mexico?"

Sixto made a grimace. "They stole

fresh animals up yonder somewhere. No horse could take the punishment they've given them. Going one way, yes, coming back, no."

The young *vaquero* was riding twisted from the waist. "I'm curious," he said.

Sixto glowered. "You are *loco*. Do you know what they do to prisoners?"

"What?"

"Stake them out on the ground naked, flesh away their eyelids and leave them. Are they gaining?"

"I can't tell. They are a long way back. Before we reach home they will be close enough to see us — Sixto?"

"What?"

"We could ambush them."

The larger, older man turned sharply as he gestured with an outflung arm. "Where? In this poor underbrush? Four against fifteen?"

Sixto urged his horse ahead, leaving the younger man to ride farther back. He occasionally peered over his shoulder. For a fact the border-jumpers were gaining. They were still too far back to close the distance before Sixto led his companions into Stillwater, but the longer Sixto watched them the more convinced he became that the border-jumpers were not going to bypass Stillwater on their way south.

For one thing, they were angling easterly on their southward route, which would take them directly toward Stillwater. He sat forward worrying about the messenger he had sent to Jawn Henry. If the town was alerted it still would not have a lot of time to prepare for an assault.

Fifteen *bandoleros* against the whole town did not make sense. There were at least fifty or sixty men in Stillwater able to fight. With adequate warning they could be prepared to blow the border-jumpers to kingdom come.

But Sixto knew Mexicans; full of *pulque* they became ten feet tall and bullet-proof.

If Jawn Henry hadn't got the warning, hadn't organized resistance, it might be different. *Bandoleros* never lingered;

they accomplished whatever was their goal and raced away. More than one town had been decimated and burned because its menfolk were taken by surprise, even when they had out-numbered the raiders five or ten to one.

Sixto was soaked with sweat when he saw rooftops. The horse under him was sucking air like a fish out of water. He eased up a little. The horse was an old friend, he would have risked his own death in order to prevent breaking the animal's wind.

He was several hundred yards behind the younger riders when he saw men moving among outbuildings with rifles and carbines. Sixto was not a praying man but he gave thanks his messenger had found Jawn Henry. Stillwater would be ready when the raiders entered the town shooting at anything that moved.

He left his animal with a small Mexican boy to take down to Mex-town for Elena to care for. Carried his saddle-gun in one big fist as he hunted the constable, who was not at his jailhouse although the roadway door was wide open.

Where they met, a dozen townsmen were trying to speak at once. Jawn Henry growled at them to get among the buildings and hold their fire, then shouldered past to face Sixto Erro. "How many?" he asked.

Sixto grounded the Winchester as he replied. "I don't know, but it don't look like any more than went north. Less than twenty by their tracks."

Jawn Henry scowled. "Are they drunk or crazy? It'd take five times that many to raid Stillwater."

Sixto shrugged, he was thirsty enough to drink swamp-water. He left the constable to find water. The moment they were no longer talking, townsmen surrounded the lawman again, all talking at once.

Jawn Henry pushed them away, went over to the west side of town where he could see the border-jumpers who were still a fair distance north but coming fast. He tried to count them and failed but they appeared to be as Sixto had said, less than twenty. On his way toward the north end of town he encountered those two old men who had given the original alarm. One was carrying a buffalo-rifle with a bore a man could stick his thumb in. He was belted around the middle, with a horse-pistol and a fleshing-knife.

His companion had a Kentucky rifle, frail-looking, with a stock of bird's-eye maple. It shot one bullet at a time but had a range greater than most long-barrelled weapons, and if properly aimed always hit its target.

One way or another Stillwater was ready!

12

The Unexpected

THE oncoming raiders did not slacken their pace but when they were close enough to be counted two of them converged, yelling back and forth. Jawn Henry thought he recognized one of them, a dark man with a six-gun balanced in his upraised right fist.

Jericho!

The *bandoleros* were travelling down the west side of town. Whether they saw the armed townsmen was doubtful, most of them were sheltered by sheds, fences, residences; but Jawn Henry gave the devil his due, these were seasoned marauders. They had to see some of the armed men watching their approach, or, if not, then they surely expected some resistance. Rarely were raiders able to attack a town or a village before someone yelled a warning. But in daylight a hard-riding, heavily-armed band of riders wearing crossed bandoliers and seen to be heading for a town meant serious trouble.

Jawn Henry shook his head, was still watching from the south side of a rattling building when Sixto came up, looked northward and said, "*Madre de Dios*, may they die here."

Jawn Henry said nothing. He was watching one of the foremost riders, a dark man whose face was finally recognizable. He was raising his Winchester when two of the raiders swerved away from the others, several of whom yelled encouragement in Spanish as the detached pair rode directly toward the easterly outskirts of Stillwater.

Jawn Henry and Sixto Erro were not the only watchers who were baffled by this.

Someone not far from where the large man and the constable were standing yelled loudly, "Shoot! Kill 'em!"

But no-one fired. The pair of charging *bandoleros* came close to several buildings on the west side while their companions continued racing southward.

"Crazy," Sixto exclaimed. *"Loco en cabeza."*

Maybe they were indeed crazy in the head, but moments later they both stood in their stirrups, hurled something as hard as they could and reined around to pursue their companions who were already nearing the lower end of town.

The explosions were deafening. None of the defenders was prepared for that. One explosion tore half the siding from a house where townsmen were crouching. The other one went farther; when it exploded it tore a hole in the main roadway north of the saloon. Its concussion broke several glass windows.

Gunfire erupted near the lower end of town. It was fierce and un-slackening.

Men from the northern areas ran southward yelling and brandishing their weapons.

The fight had bypassed Jawn Henry and Sixto, who hurried down the alley toward the sound of gunfire. Now, the raiders were firing back. Glass shattered, wooden siding splintered, somewhere a woman screamed for her son to get back inside. The smell of burnt powder was strong, but above all else was the noise. The townsmen at the lower end of town were unrelenting despite the furious return-fire of the raiders, two of whom went down in a wild tumble, their horses having been shot from beneath them. One *bandolero* slackened almost to a stop and stood in his stirrups with an upraised right arm. The bullet that hit him came from a rifle that made a sharper, higher-pitched report than most rifles. The raider went off the far side of his horse and moments later the little hand-bomb he had been trying to throw exploded. The man had been in the drag of his companions but the explosion knocked several horses to their knees, steel fragments struck a *bandolero* in the back. He bent far over to grasp mane hair, missed, struck the ground and bounced.

One horse bogged his head and bucked for all he was worth. His rider, light in the stirrup, was flung off and landed on his head. He squirmed briefly then lay still with a broken neck.

The raiders were badly decimated and the survivors were widening the distance with spurs and curses. In the lead a raider was astride what seemed to be a thoroughbred; at least the animal was tall with a long stride. He was leaving his nearest companions well behind when an old man stood up, locked one hand on a piece of siding, aimed with full concentration and squeezed the trigger with his other hand.

The tall horse ran out from under his rider. The man seemed to hang suspended in the air for seconds before falling face down. There was blood on the back and front of his jacket, up high.

Jawn Henry squinted for a sighting of Jericho. Now there was dust as well as pandemonium. Sixto tapped his arm and pointed. The raider who had taken the place of the man who had been shot off his race-horse was the only surviving raider not riding a Mexican saddle.

Jawn Henry took an arm-rest as old Herb had done when he'd shot the raider off the tall horse, eased back the dog and hunched to aim as Sixto said, "Too far. Hurry up."

Jawn Henry allowed for elevation and squeezed the trigger. The hard-rider out front did not even flinch. Sixto was disgusted. "Damned carbine's no good for distance. Come along!"

They hastened to the lower end of town, entered the livery-barn down there, did not see the liveryman, who was in the back alley with other shooters. They appropriated two stalled animals, rigged them out in a hurry, sprang astride, rode up to the roadway and headed south.

Defenders recognized both mounted men, called back and forth for shooters to hold their fire. One man, short, bull-built and fog-horn-voiced, yelled, "Get horses!" His shout sent men racing every which way, some to their private stables, others to the livery-barn.

The raiders did not ease up nor look back. They had lost half their band. They had miscalculated the number of defenders lined up among the shelters on the west side of town as they had raced past less than fifty yards out.

It hadn't exactly been a turkey-shoot but it had come close. There were a number of horses bearing Mexican saddles running in all directions.

The fight was over almost before it got started. The raiders had never slackened speed. Their intention had not been to attack the town, but to ride past and hurl their little bombs, the objective evidently being to frighten the whey out of folks. If indeed that had been their intention they had succeeded. Most of the townsfolk had never seen a bomb in their lives let alone have two explode in their town.

Jawn Henry and Sixto Erro rode low and fast, each with a six-gun in his fist. The livery animals they had appropriated would ordinarily not have been in the same league with the horses of the *bandoleros*, except that the raiders had been pushing their animals hard since leaving Tres Pinos; horseflesh had limits. The raiders could have reached the border and crossed it if they had favoured their animals, but after the attack on Stillwater they had no choice but to punish their mounts in order to stay alive.

Jawn Henry was within six-gun range when a desperate marauder whose animal was giving out, suddenly yanked to a halt and raised his carbine. Both Sixto and Jawn Henry fired at the same time. The raider was going off his horse from impact when he squeezed the trigger. The bullet went skyward as the raider's horse tucked up, spun and raced back the way he had come, steel stirrups flapping, braided reins flying. He passed Jawn Henry and Sixto from a distance of less than forty feet, eyes glazed with irrational fear.

Sixto shouted. "Five left," and hooked his livery animal.

Jawn Henry offered no reply. He was concentrating on a man astride an exceptionally durable horse who was steadily out-distancing them all. The rider was sitting half-twisted from the waist looking back. Jawn Henry would have known that face anywhere on earth between heaven and hell.

The distance was too great for a handgun. Jawn Henry had left his carbine leaning in the livery-barn. If he'd had it he probably could not have downed Jericho; the range was not too great, although it was a goodly distance for accurate shooting, but the back of a running horse was about the poorest place for anyone to shoot from.

A raider veered westerly on his ailing horse. He twisted and got off a shot that came close enough for Sixto to roar a curse and turn aside in pursuit.

Jericho had three raiders behind him. One, a thick man with one of the ubiquitous Mexican machetes bouncing along on the right side of his saddle, dry-fired his six-gun twice, hurled it at Jawn Henry with a roared curse and spun back reaching for his machete. Jawn Henry shot the man through the body before he could raise the big knife. The raider dropped the machete, grabbed his oversized saddle-horn with both hands, lost his reins and was bent double as his frightened horse carried him back toward Stillwater.

Jawn Henry was close enough to finish him off but refrained from wasting a bullet. He did not have a full load in his handgun as it was, and the gut-shot marauder did not need another bullet.

One of the raiders behind Jericho suddenly left his speeding horse in a flying leap, landed hard, rolled over, sprang to his feet with both arms above his head.

Jawn Henry flashed past, got about ten yards when the man yanked a six-gun from under his charro jacket in back and fired. Jawn Henry heard the gun go off, felt something like the sting of a wasp and did not look back. The bullet had shredded the lobe of his right ear, which bled furiously, drenching his shirt and sleeve on the right side down to the cuff.

An old ragged scarecrow riding a sway-back mule hauled his animal to a halt, stumbled from the saddle, raised his ancient hexagonal-barrelled buffalo-gun and fired. Smoke erupted, the recoil almost knocked old Sam Mortenson on his back. Where the thumb-sized slug hit the raider everything, shirting, flesh and bone exploded in a scarlet froth.

The townsmen who saw this nearly halted. The old man swore at them while massaging his shoulder. "You gawddamned fish-livered bastards, go after 'em. *Go, damn you!*"

The mob of townsmen ran past the old man, who ignored his victim, sat on the ground with his nearby mule looking woebegone, gazing at his heavy old rifle lying in the dirt. "That's the last time, consarn you. Thirty years back you liked to broke my shoulder ten times. This time I think you did break it."

He was still sitting there when his friend came up, halted, leaned on his saddle-horn and said, "I been tellin' you for twenty years to get shed of that gun an' get yourself somethin' that don't half-kill a man when he shoots it."

"I never wanted no other gun, you blasted screwt. Help me up."

Herb dismounted awkwardly, hitched at his sagging britches and moved to help his friend as he said, "We're too old for this."

"Just help me get back on the mule."

As he grunted his friend upright the

old man looked at the dead raider. "What'n hell did you load into that gun, Sam?"

"I don't know. I ain't shot it in twenty, thirty years. Back then we used buffler-loads." Sam held up his thumb. "Broke off a chunk of lead about this size, smoothed it . . . Hold that damned mule still, will you!"

They were alone, the townsmen were far ahead. Even farther ahead two raiders were gouging their horses for everything they had left, which was not enough. One raider raked his horse hard when the animal stumbled. The horse managed another couple of hundred feet before folding its front legs and going down, pitching its rider ahead. He lost his six-gun.

The townsmen swarmed around him. The raider was dazed, otherwise he might have looked for the gun he had lost. Four townsmen piled off, yanked him to his feet, went over him for hideout weapons, found a dagger, belly-gun and a wicked-bladed clasp-knife, which they appropriated.

The Mexican had a split lip and a swelling eye.

He was young, no more perhaps than his late teens or early twenties. He hadn't been a raider long enough to glare and curse.

They put him behind a townsman's saddle, made a cordon around him and started back to town. All but three unrelenting townsmen continued the pursuit, but they had wasted too much time. Jawn Henry and Jericho, with the only surviving *bandolero* beside the 'breed, were a long mile ahead.

Jawn Henry saw the tall horse stumble several times but before that happened the last raider who was trying to keep up with Jericho bailed off his horse and rolled frantically into an arroyo. His horse did as another horse had done, he reversed himself and went back in the direction of Stillwater, but at a very slow, shambling lope.

Jawn Henry had no illusions, the livery animal he was straddling was no better than an average horse, neither well-reined nor fast. The only element in his favour was that while he was sucking air, the tall horse ahead was giving out as a result of hard use over many times as many miles as Jawn Henry's horse had been ridden.

Jericho might have had a Winchester. There was a boot on the right-hand side of his saddle, but it was empty. What Jericho did have was a six-gun, which he fired twice, twisting from the waist to do so. Both bullets went far wide.

Jawn Henry did not fire back. He slackened off a little until his mount was no more than loping.

Jericho faced forward, swung his head from side to side. There were no arroyos on either side, at least not close enough for him to reach.

He twisted to shoot again. This time the slug was close enough to tug at Jawn Henry's sleeve and tear it without drawing blood. Still Jawn Henry did not fire back.

Jericho looped both reins, shoved the six-gun into his waistband and twisted to claw frantically at the pair of saddlebags on either side of his saddle behind the cantle.

Jawn Henry guessed Jericho intended to hurl the saddlebags backward to divert the constable's horse, which was indeed what the renegade had in mind but in a way Jawn Henry would never have guessed.

When he had both saddlebags freed he unbuckled one, stood in his stirrups and hurled both saddlebags directly in Jawn Henry's path.

The livery horse did not shy at the sight of the leather pouches coming at him, but he did miss a lead as a shower of greenbacks fluttered in the air, dozens of them, almost a shower of money.

Jericho hunched forward and raked his horse to take advantage of the confusion he had caused, but the reason he had showered Jawn Henry with money from the bank up at Tres

Pinos had not been entirely to cause the livery animal to shy. It had been to give Jawn Henry time to have second thoughts about stopping to gather up all that money, more money in fact than Jawn Henry had ever seen before in his life.

If it hadn't been for the blood-feud between them, Jawn Henry might have been diverted, which was something that would never be satisfactorily answered, and something some folks would call Jawn Henry a damned fool for not taking advantage of.

Jawn Henry ignored the blizzard of greenbacks, concentrated on the fleeing man ahead — and his giving-out saddle-animal.

Jericho fired once more from the hurricane deck of the ailing horse, and as before Jawn Henry did not fire back.

The horse-race ended when Jericho's horse stumbled over a large rock and fell like a sack of wet grain. He was bordering on being wind-broke and except for his fall he probably would have continued to run another mile or two until he was wind broke — for which the only remedy was a bullet in the head.

As it was, the horse would recover. It would require months but he would eventually recover fully. But when he fell and flung Jericho off, the 'breed got up.

He took a wide-legged stance facing back. This time he used both hands to steady his aimed six-gun. Jawn Henry took the only course available to him, he ducked low behind the head and neck of the livery-animal.

There was no explosion. Jawn Henry was closing the distance when he saw Jericho haul back the dog for another shot, and this time Jawn Henry saw the hammer fall on another spent casing.

He did not slacken the livery-horse when he came abreast of the 'breed; he hurled himself from the saddle, struck Jericho hard enough to knock half the wind out of him, and rolled on hard ground with both hands gripping the renegade.

Jericho fought like a tiger. He was sweaty, panting and wild-eyed. He fought for his life. Jawn Henry tried unsuccessfully to hold both Jericho's wrists. He took a fist high in the face, slightly above and between both eyes.

For five seconds Jawn Henry could only push his face into the 'breed's chest and hang on. His mind cleared, his grip tightened until he could yank the lighter man half off the ground and hit him hard alongside the jaw.

Jericho went limp all over.

Jawn Henry sat in the dirt beside his unconscious enemy. His heart was pounding, he was gulping air and his head hurt.

Jericho's horse had regained his feet. He and Jawn Henry's livery-animal were standing side by side, head-hung-exhausted. There was no sign of the town-riders and Sixto was two miles away with another pair of horses standing in bone-weary exhaustion. At

Sixto's feet was a *bandolero* dead as a stone with two purplish puckers in his head, one on each side.

Jericho moaned and made scrabbling claw-marks in the dust. Jawn Henry rolled him over. Jericho rolled back and got to his knees, hung there like a gut-shot bear for several minutes before turning his head. He looked steadily at Jawn Henry and spoke thickly. "You brainless bastard. There was five thousand dollars in them saddlebags. You could live easy for ten years."

Jawn Henry arose, beat dust off and told the 'breed to stand up.

Jericho had to be helped. When he was upright Jawn Henry stepped away, expecting Jericho to collapse. He had hit him hard, hard enough to put larger, tougher men down and keep them down.

Jericho lurched, caught himself, put a hand up to the swelling on the lower side of his face. His gaze at Jawn Henry was cold. He seemed about to speak again. Jawn Henry expected him to and was watching his face when Jericho's dazed clumsiness vanished in a twinkling and his free hand came up with a single-shot, slightly made, almost delicate-looking belly-gun with a barrel no more than two inches long.

Jawn Henry's surprise did not interfere with his reflexes. He lashed out with his left hand, punched Jericho off balance, and went for the Colt in the front of his britches with his right hand.

Both guns went off almost simultaneously; the slug from the little hideout weapon threw dirt over Jawn Henry's boot, his bullet hit the 'breed low and passed completely through. Jericho went down in a heap. He gasped and struggled to roll over to get back upright. The lower half of his body would not respond.

Jawn Henry stood over the renegade, thumb-pad on the knurled hammer to draw it back and fire again.

Jericho stopped twisting and looked up. "You're lucky. Just lucky. Help me up."

Jawn Henry shoved the Colt back into his waistband without offering the renegade a hand.

Instead, he knelt beside him. "Your back's broke."

"Quit squirming. Just lie still."

They were on the ground beside one another for almost a full fifteen minutes without speaking before Jericho made a slight rattling sound and looked steadily upwards. Jawn Henry waited another ten minutes, until he saw the dryness in the dead man's eyes, then got wearily to his feet, brought the horses over, hoisted Jericho across his saddle, lashed him in place, mounted the livery-animal and started back.

He scarcely noticed the scattered greenbacks or the still-buckled right-side saddlebag.

By the time he reached Stillwater the dead raiders had been brought to town and placed in a sitting position out front of the harness-works where the emporium owner had set up a camera and had taken their picture.

He did not get them all. Sixto left his dead raider where the man had died. One raider was never accounted for although curious townsmen found sign where a man had hidden in an arroyo on his way south on foot.

Three days after the dead had been planted some townsmen from Tres Pinos arrived in Stillwater with the story of how the raiders had come into the town close to dusk when folks were at supper, used some kind of little bomb to blow open the bank and its safe, taken all the money in the vault — nine thousand dollars — and shot four people who had come outside when the explosions occurred.

Jawn Henry gave them the money and the saddlebags it had been in. He stood them a round at the saloon and saw them on their way out of town.

He and Sixto sat in *ramada* shade down in Mex-town speaking quietly and carefully. For one thing Sixto had killed his raider when the man had lost his sidearm; one of those things a man could feel justified in doing but never talked about, not even to a close friend.

Jawn Henry's equal circumspection had a similar basis. In thinking back, he hadn't had to kill Jericho. After pushing him enough for the renegade to miss Jawn Henry and plough dirt with his belly-gun, Jawn Henry could simply have knocked him senseless again.

Stillwater was to become, to later generations, the site of a courageous triumph over border-jumping marauders whose number increased considerably over the years. Many years later someone collected a comfortable donation around town, had a fine plaque made telling the story of the Stillwater Raid in lurid detail.

When Sixto and Jawn Henry appeared for the unveiling they exchanged an impassive long look and headed for the cantina in Mex-town. The only accurate statement on the plaque was the date.

TOP HAND
Wade Everett

The Broken T was big. But no ranch is big enough to let a man hide from himself.

GUN WOLVES OF LOBO BASIN
Lee Floren

The Feud was a blood debt. When Smoke Talbot found the outlaws who gunned down his folks he aimed to nail their hide to the barn door.

SHOTGUN SHARKEY
Marshall Grover

The westbound coach carrying the indomitable Larry and Stretch headed for a shooting showdown.

FIGHTING RAMROD
Charles N. Heckelmann

Most men would have cut their losses, but Frazer counted the bullets in his guns and said he'd soak the range in blood before he'd give up another inch of what was his.

LONE GUN
Eric Allen

Smoke Blackbird had been away too long. The Lequires had seized the Blackbird farm, forcing the Indians and settlers off, and no one seemed willing to fight! He had to fight alone.

THE THIRD RIDER
Barry Cord

Mel Rawlins wasn't going to let anything stand in his way. His father was murdered, his two brothers gone. Now Mel rode for vengeance.

ARIZONA DRIFTERS
W. C. Tuttle

When drifting Dutton and Lonnie Steelman decide to become partners they find that they have a common enemy in the formidable Thurston brothers.

TOMBSTONE
Matt Braun

Wells Fargo paid Luke Starbuck to outgun the silver-thieving stagecoach gang at Tombstone. Before long Luke can see the only thing bearing fruit in this eldorado will be the gallows tree.

HIGH BORDER RIDERS
Lee Floren

Buckshot McKee and Tortilla Joe cut the trail of a border tough who was running Mexican beef into Texas. They stopped the smuggler in his tracks.